THIS TIME FOREVER

Hope you enjoy!
Best, Mary

Mary Cooney-Glazer

This Time Forever

Published by Mary Cooney-Glazer
Printed in the United States of America
ISBN: 0999247808
ISBN 13: 9780999247808

DISCLAIMER: *This Time Forever is a work of fiction. Names, characters, places
and events are either the product of the author's imagination or are used fictitiously.
Any resemblance to actual persons, living or dead, or to actual events is entirely
coincidental.*

Contact: Mary Cooney-Glazer
Email: mcgbooks@aol.com

DEDICATION

This book is dedicated to my husband, Myles Glazer, Ph.D.

We were lucky to meet when we had enough experience in the world of singledom to be as sure as one can be about another.

After over three decades of marriage, we're ready to say it was probably a good match.

Myles has been understanding and supportive about *This Time Forever* coming before almost everything else in our lives.

I could never have finished this without his love and encouragement.

SPECIAL THANKS

Without a wonderful group of talented, helpful, patient, and supportive people I would never have completed this novel. Here's my warm and special expression of gratitude.

My beta readers gave helpful comments on the plot and the characters. They wielded their red pens carefully to correct errors. Judith Carroll Evans, and Heidi Kaufman Klein, thank you for your comments and for your meticulous attention to punctuation, spelling, and matters of grammar.

Diane Rapalyea, thank you for being my cheerleader and for all the reassurance during times I felt this would not happen.

Thank you to members of my writing group, North Shore Scribes.

Lina Rehal encouraged me to write this first novel. She is the published author of *Loving Daniel*, a romance novel, *October in New*

York, a romance novella, and *Carousel Kisses,* a collection of nostalgic vignettes about growing up in the late fifties. The books are available from Amazon.

Lina has been my mentor, editor, technical and art consultant, alpha reader, beta reader and a source of ongoing encouragement. Thank you, Lina. *This Time Forever* would not be a published novel without you.

Last, but no less sincerely, thank you to all the people who have endured endless chatter from me about this book. I feel safe in assuming the subject wasn't the only thing you wanted to discuss, day and night. I appreciate your indulgence.

Mary

TABLE OF CONTENTS

CHAPTER 1
THEY MEET

ANGIE

As Angie drove just a bit over the speed limit, she could feel her red hair drying into an uncontrolled curly mass. *That's what I get for leaving the house just out of the shower. But why would I worry about impressing anyone at the mall today? As long as my charge card is good, who'll care how I look?*

She parked her BMW, and stuffed the keys in a deep pocket of her old faded jeans. Just inside the store, she pulled out a shopping list, then fished reading glasses out of her black tee shirt pocket. *Damn! I need these things to read everything lately.*

The salesclerk in the linen department didn't smile or respond to a friendly "Hi." Angie continued, "I'm looking for the yellow towels advertised on sale in this ad."

Not moving, the woman responded, "Well, if they're not out, we don't have them in yellow."

"OK, I'll just order them and you can have them sent."

"You could do that on-line you know."

"Yes, I could, but I'm here, and you have the computer up." She was trying to keep the edge out of her voice.

"Oh, all right then," the clerk said grudgingly.

Angie noticed the tall coffee next to the register. "If you get to it, your coffee will still be hot when you finish." *Crap! That was snarky and I need this woman to send the damn towels to my house, not to East Bejeezus somewhere.*

There was a muffled laugh behind her, but she was too irritated to care that somebody appreciated her subtle sarcasm.

She signed the sales slip, gave a civil thank you, and took a long step back, turning at the same time.

The man in back of her couldn't move fast enough to avoid a collision. He kept Angie from falling as she plowed into the middle of his chest.

"Oh my god, that was my fault. I am so sorry. Are you OK?" Angie was mortified as he held her shoulders until she was safely balanced upright. She apologized while she steadied herself, before seeing his face.

"I'm fine," he answered, "No worries." Then, "I knew that voice, but I couldn't believe it!" he said. "Angela, is it really you?"

There was only one man in the world who called her by her full name and made it sound that wonderful.

She stood there, barely keeping herself composed.

I should say no, wrong person. Then I should run as fast as I can away from here. He's still wearing the same cologne. The one that made me cry whenever I smelled it for years after we split.

"It's been well over twenty years, and I'd know you anywhere," Ben told her, adding, "You're still beautiful."

Her thoughts raced.

That sexy British accent is still there. How can he look as good with gray hair as he did when he was blond? I felt solid muscle

2

when I bumped into him. Why couldn't he be fat and old looking? Oh god, did I at least remember to put on lipstick? What the hell is he doing in a linen department in Peabody? Why am I hesitating? I need to go. Now!

Red alerts flashed, and alarms were sounding in her brain. She ignored all of them.

I cannot believe I'm feeling this way!

Angie was afraid her voice would shake, so she just smiled and offered her hand. A moment later she managed to say "Hello, Ben," while memories came rushing in like dammed water when the floodgates opened.

It was all so long ago. We were planning a life together, then, he went home to London for a week. That weekend before he left was the last time we saw each other.

There was only the one terrible phone call. Ben hadn't let her get further than "Hello" when he spoke. The conversation etched itself in her brain.

"Angela, I am so sorry. It's over between us. I thought it would work, but I can't commit to you. I'm not returning to the US. Please don't try to contact me. I won't respond. Goodbye."

The line was disconnected before she could say a word.

Now, here was Ben, again, twenty-four years later, in the linen department of Springer's. He had the same wonderful smile, and he was looking at Angie as if she were the only person in the world.

Why am I not furious with him? Why do I still want to know what happened? Why am I acting like a damn fool?

Angie decided not to look for reasons.

❦

BEN

Ben froze on the spot when he heard the tall redhead in front of him sparring with the reluctant sales clerk. He knew she was Angela, the only woman he had ever loved. Now she was standing in the linen department of Springer's, not a foot away from him.

This cannot be happening. But it is. I'd know that voice anywhere. I have to speak to her.

Thoughts were thundering through his head. He hoped she wouldn't scream at him, or worse, walk away without a word. *She'd have every right to do either, after the way I left her.*

Miraculously, by stepping back so fast, she gave him the opportunity not only to speak to her, but to hold her as well. He wanted to wrap her in a hug.

He listened to her embarrassed apology, smiling at the concern in her voice that she might have hurt him. Ben reassured her he was fine. *The way her mouth opened a bit in surprise, I know she recognizes my voice as well. She looks like she might want to bolt, but for some reason, she isn't. Angela damn well remembers everything about us. I can see it in her eyes.*

He noticed it took her a few seconds to speak, then, after calmly saying, "Hello Ben," she smiled, looked relaxed, and listened to him tell her how he would recognize her anywhere.

I hope I'm making some kind of sense and not babbling like a fool. I screwed up royally twenty-four years ago. Angela is still lovely, with her curly hair and those expressive brown eyes. I know she married after we split. She's not wearing a ring, but that doesn't mean anything. Women like her are rarely on their own for any length of time.

I wonder if it took her as long as I needed to get on with life after our break-up? Because it damn near killed me. Hell, I never really got over it. I loved her so much. At the time, I was crazy enough to think there wasn't another choice. Never gave her a chance to make her own decision about things.

What a bloody idiot I am to hope she'd consider spending a few minutes with me. But I'll regret it for the rest of my life if I don't try.

⇌

BOTH OF THEM

They asked together. "Coffee?"

Then, laughing, answered in unison, "Sure."

"May I help you, Sir?" The suddenly helpful sales clerk interrupted them.

"Angela, do you mind if I pick up a couple of things before we go?"

"Of course not."

"I'd like two sets of cream-color queen-size sheets with pillow cases, please."

Wouldn't he have a king sized bed if he were sharing it? She mentally shook herself. *That's none of your damn business! We're going for a quick coffee. We'll probably bore each other within twenty minutes.* She squashed an intruding thought. *So, who're you trying to kid?*

She remembered her double bed had been short for his six-foot three height. He never complained though. She blushed a little, thinking that back then, they'd have done fine with a twin.

He watched Angela standing quietly. *Wonder how she's feeling? What she's remembering? Get over yourself, Mate, she's probably just being polite. Don't put too much stock into having coffee. But she did ask too...has it been long enough for what I did not to matter much anymore?*

Finished with his purchase, he thanked the clerk and turned to Angie.

"So, do you have a favorite coffee place? Somewhere they'll let us sit and talk for a while without hovering?"

She remembered the plant-filled atrium on the lower level of the mall. They could get coffee from the kiosk there and sit as long as they liked. *It's a pleasant space, but open. Not the least bit intimate. Anyone can see us.*

"Sure, Ben. I think you'll like it."

CHAPTER 2
COFFEE

B en glanced at Angela as often as he could without being obvious as they strolled through the mall. He barely stopped himself from taking her hand.

She allowed herself to enjoy walking with him at her side. *I know it's dumb to do this, but we're only having coffee in a public place.*

"Do you like to shop, Ben?"

"No, I mostly do it on-line. Sometimes, though, I want to gauge the heft of a piece of furniture. I like to feel the softness of a material if I'm going to sleep on it too."

Angela blushed a bit when he mentioned the softness of things next to his skin. She remembered that he was always sensitive to how things felt. He loved it when she wore silk and lace.

Why the blush? Ben wondered. *What was she thinking about? Hell, don't be stupid. It's bloody humid in here, and Angela never liked heat.* Then he remembered how she blushed when they made love. *Don't even go there, you idiot. This is coffee. She might never want to see you again.*

7

"I usually wait until I am desperate for things," Angela broke into his thoughts. "When I finally do get to a mall, it's early in the day, before the crowds. I'm not a recreational shopper. Except in bookstores. I can hang out in them for hours."

Ben smiled to himself. He loved books as well. Then, in what seemed like seconds, they were on an escalator down to the coffee bar.

She led him into a sunny space, punctuated with potted hibiscus, Norfolk Island Pines, and an occasional palm. The low tables with comfortable easy chairs were scattered amid the greenery, so that each had a little buffer of privacy.

Angela headed to a corner, visible to the rest of the room, but a bit more secluded.

"This spot good for you, Ben?"

"Sure, let me drop these bags and I'll get us some coffee."

As he hurried off, Ben thought, *she picked a table where we can talk comfortably, but not good for any emotional discussion. Maybe she's not interested in the past. Well, somehow, sometime, I'm going to find a way to tell her why I hurt her so badly. She has a right to know it wasn't her fault.*

From his place in line, he saw Angela on her cell. *Who's she talking to? She's smiling, turned to the side as if she wants whatever she's saying to be very private. Is she calling her husband, or someone else who has a claim on her time?*

Ben recognized a little possessiveness in his thought. *You really are an ass. You have no right to feel anything but apologetic to Angela. You don't even know how she drinks her coffee.* Then he remembered. *She disliked paper cups. She wanted a touch, not more than that, of cream. She loved the aroma, but didn't like it too strong.*

They used to enjoy outdoor cafes in the morning on weekends. The coffee was a ritual after a night of romance, and then, if he was lucky, a warm, slow shower together. He loved to wash her hair, and, for that matter, every part of her.

"How can I help you, Sir?" The slightly impatient barista interrupted Ben's reverie. *How long was I standing here daydreaming?*

He arrived back with a full tray, carrying everything he could think of to satisfy any way Angela wanted coffee. There was cream, milk, sugar, sweetener, a pot of hot water, two scones on a plate, butter, jelly, knives, spoons and napkins.

She laughed, softly. "Oh Ben! This looks like something I'd get at the Ritz! You covered every base."

"I wanted to be sure that you were happy with my waitering, Ma'am," he joked back. *And I wanted to impress you, too.*

Angie thanked him. "You remembered I like real mugs! How thoughtful. But I drink it black now. We traveled a lot, and it was just easier. The coffee here is full-bodied though, so having hot water is perfect."

We traveled a lot. Who's the we? And why the past tense?

He put the tray on the table between them. They sipped coffee and buttered the scones before starting to talk. Ben picked up on travel. He thought it might be a casual way to find out more about her life.

"So, tell me a couple of your favorite destinations." He smiled, his hazel eyes watching her intently.

Dammit! Why did I bring up travel? I'm not here for a light and pointless chat. It might be stupid, but even after all these years, I want to know what happened to us. Still, maybe it's not such a bad way to learn more about him without seeming nosey. Might give me a clue about what I want to find out.

"Alaska and Italy." Her answer came fast, because she loved both places. *I'm sure as hell not telling him England, where I thought he lived, even though it's on top of the list of places I enjoy.*

"I get to Italy now and again too, Angela. I love Tuscany."

"Oh, that's one of my favorite areas!" She nearly bit her tongue for blurting that out.

"We seem to like some of the same places."

"A few, anyway." She sounded dismissive. "Do you still spend most of your time in London, Ben?"

"Not anymore. I consider the US to be as much my home as England now. I've lived most of the time here for a while."

"Really." She responded casually, but her face tightened a bit.

"I'm in this area to help get a house in Cambridge organized. I bought it for my boys. They're both in grad school, one at Harvard, the other at MIT. It's three floors and they're living there as we speak. My digs aren't ready yet. Luckily, a friend in Plover Cove needed someone to condo-sit for a month. It worked out."

Angela's smile felt false to her. She couldn't imagine why she was so startled that Ben fell in love, married, and had children.

CHAPTER 3
STILL WONDERING

He must have met the woman almost immediately after he dumped me, if I'm guessing the right ages for the kids. So much for my idiotic fantasy that some great tragedy forced him to break up with me.

Ben saw surprise, anger, and hurt in her eyes. *Oh my god! I really blundered that bit. She probably thinks I left because of another woman I had stashed in London. Better fix things now, before she runs off.*

"My boys, Ryan and Pete, are adopted. I was a single dad for several years. It's a long story, Angela, with a horrific start. They required a great deal of time and attention, and I had to make some very difficult choices. There wasn't room for much else but work, I'm afraid. Thankfully, they both grew up to be wonderful young men. Life without them is unimaginable now."

How old are these kids? Why did he adopt them? Did that have anything to do with what happened to us? Angie's eyes never left his face.

"That had to be a challenge, having an instant family." She was remembering the man she knew twenty-four years ago, carefree, ambitious, and a bit selfish about how he spent his time. Yet, he was loving, kind, and fiercely protective.

He took time to warm his coffee with hot water before answering.

"Yes, it certainly was. Mostly, we all adapted reasonably well. However, there were some chaotic and very emotional times at first."

She kept her expression neutral. *I sure as hell know about emotional chaos. I cried all night for months after you left.*

"And now you're all living in the states?"

"Yes. We can travel back and forth as we wish though. We're citizens of both countries."

He continued to give her a bare bones version of his life, saying he had been divorced for eight years, but that it had been friendly.

"Now, what about you Angela?"

She told him she had married Dan Wilson twenty-one years before and moved from Boston to Rock Harbor.

"He was a widower, sixteen years older than I. Both of us decided it would be good to start our life together somewhere interesting, without old memories. Rock Harbor seemed to fit the bill. We enjoyed the town and made great friends."

"Dan died three years ago." Her eyes teared.

Ben reached over and took her hand. "I am very sorry, Angela."

"Thank you. He was skiing, and had a massive heart attack. Didn't suffer. It was good for him, but a terrible shock for everyone else. I miss him. However, work and wonderful friends make life busy and enjoyable."

She had left her hand in his while telling him about her husband's death, then gently moved it to get a handkerchief from her purse.

It must have been awful to lose someone she loved for a second time. But, selfish as it is, I'm so glad she's single...or at least not married. He was feeling an attraction as powerful as it was unreasonable. However, there was no denying it was real.

"Well, we've both seen our share of good and bad over the years, haven't we?" Ben's eyes were soft and sympathetic as he smiled gently at her.

I'm so confused! This man hurt me beyond belief. Yet, I love talking to him. I feel almost as if we've been friends for life. But nobody who cared about me would do what he did, no matter what. How could I ever trust him again? Not that I'll ever have to worry about that.

"Coffee's cold. Shall we have another, Angela?"

Her cell phone rang with an urgent siren-like sound before she could answer. "Oh Ben, I have to get this. It's my emergency on-call ring. I am sorry"

Angie dug through her large handbag, saying, "I don't get why they're calling today. I'm officially off duty and one of my associates is covering. This must be something urgent." She pulled an envelope and a wallet out, left both on the table, then grabbed her phone. When she saw the number, she stood. "Excuse me a minute. It's about a client, I'm sure."

What kind of clients does she have that they'd be allowed to contact her when she's not working? Ben wondered.

Angela had moved several tables away, out of earshot, but he could see her. *From the look on her face and her posture, I'm sure we're finished with coffee. I don't even know her married name or where she lives, but I can't let this chance go.*

He pulled out a thick linen business card, crossed out the printed contact information and wrote a cell number and email. Both were private, and only his sons had them. Angela was still talking. She looked serious. He looked at the letter and her wallet on the table.

The wallet probably has her license, but I wouldn't open it. That would be an awful thing to do. She might catch me anyway.

He turned the letter over, and saw a return address in the corner. *Ms. Angela Martin-Wilson, 175 Terrace Road, Rock Harbor, MA 01954. OK.* Scribbling the information on another business card, he tucked it in his pocket and stood as she returned to the table.

"Oh Ben, I have to go right now. It's an urgent issue that I need to manage personally. This has been a delightful reunion."

"Angela," Ben interrupted, "Can we meet again? It seems a shame not to finish catching up, but I'll leave it completely up to you." *Unless you don't call. Then I'll coax and cajole until you agree.* "Please, take my card. Use the handwritten information. You name the time and the place, and it'll be fine with me."

Angie looked straight at Ben as she moved to leave. "Well, today was pleasant, Ben. However, there's no guarantee we'll get along as well if we see each other again."

"I'll take a chance, Angela. Please, tell me your married name."

"Oh, I kept the Martin and added Dan's. It's Martin-Wilson. My email is *amw175@rockmail.com.* Can you remember?"

"Yes, I think so. Don't forget your wallet and papers."

"Oh, thanks. I would have." She kissed his cheek lightly. "Bye Ben. We'll be in touch."

He stayed watching as she hurried through the glass doors of the atrium and trotted up the little hill toward the parking area. Ben couldn't recall any woman leaving him flat, ever, no matter what was going on. He thought there might be other firsts with Angela.

CHAPTER 4

THE EMERGENCY

A ngie sensed Ben watching through the wide atrium windows. She walked quickly up an incline toward the car, puffing just a tiny bit. Beads of perspiration gathered on her forehead.

How juvenile is this, trying to show him I'm in such good shape? Should I have explained more about why I needed to leave so suddenly? No. It's good for him to wonder. And to realize I have things in my life that are more important than being with a long-ago lover who left me. It'll be at least a week before I call him, if I even bother. However, on a level deeper than conscious thought, she knew she had to see Ben again.

As hard as it was, Angie filed the morning's adventure in the back of her mind and gave full attention to what was ahead. She made herself as professional looking as she could, slipping on a tailored blazer that was always in the car. Black patent flats replaced the ratty sandals. Angie felt an appropriate appearance was important when she met clients and other people involved with them.

The call interrupting her coffee with Ben was from the ER at Seaside Hospital. Jake Acheson, her 80-year-old ex-Navy Chief neighbor, was brought in by ambulance after a fall on the sidewalk. According to the ambulance drivers, he had lost consciousness for a minute or two. Jake had her card in his wallet, clipped to his driver's license. They couldn't find a phone or any other emergency contact numbers on him. An ER nurse called her from his bedside.

Angie could hear him disagreeing, loudly and profanely, with the doctor who told him he needed to stay for tests and observation for a few hours. "Dammit Doc, this isn't the first time I've taken a crack to my noggin. It's no big deal," he said.

Jake took Angie under his wing after her husband died. He was a scourge to everyone working on her house, making sure everything was done to his specifications. He was available to wait for deliveries when Angie was working. Jake was a talented cook as well, and they ate together at least once a week.

In return, Angie accompanied him to important medical appointments. She made sure his doctors were all on the same page, and kept a discreet eye on him if he was under the weather.

"Honey," Jake told Angie once, "I know this is what you do for a living, and you charge big bucks doing whatever you call it. I can pay, you know."

"Jake, we're friends. If you paid me, then I'd have to pay you for the general contracting, security and chef's dinners. That'd probably cost more than my Nurse Concierge services. Let's just call it even, OK?"

He had a partner who should have been his first emergency contact, but Jake never updated the information. Two years before, he had told Angie, "I don't want to worry her with my medical stuff. Eileen's my love, Honey. No need to have her thinking of me as a sick old codger she needs to take care of."

"OK, Jake. I get that," she said. "But you two are pretty serious about each other. It would be a good idea to add her to your emergency list at some point."

"I'll get around to it, Honey." He never did.

This was the first time that he was in the hospital though. Angie was concerned for her friend. He was diagnosed with diabetes a year ago. Jake got all the information he could about managing it and had avoided problems. He walked at least a mile a day and usually ate well.

I wonder if he took his meds, then decided to walk downtown for breakfast? His blood sugar could have dropped. But, he might have fallen for some other reason as well.

Angie pulled into an empty space, dashed into the ER and spoke to the young man at the desk. "A nurse called me about Jake Acheson. I think he's been here for a bit over an hour."

"Are you a relative, Ma'am?" the admitting clerk asked.

"No, I'm Angela Martin-Wilson, here's my card. I'm a private Nurse Concierge and Mr. Acheson is a client." The clerk looked doubtful. "I'll need to check with my supervisor to make sure I can let you in."

"Angie, I'm so glad to see you." Joan, the ER Nurse Manager, greeted her. She turned to the concerned clerk. "It's fine, Jimmy. Angie has had several clients here before.

She's a Registered Nurse who owns Nurse Concierge Services, Inc. It's a company that helps people get through the medical system. Her clients have given signed permission allowing us to share information and let her be with them during exams and tests." "Jimmy's new, Angie. He'll get to know you."

"Come with me," the nurse led her down the hall. "Jake's not happy. He's threatening to leave against medical advice, and the doc wants to get a head C-T scan. There's a good-sized forehead bump and, when they brought him in, he was a little confused about what happened. The EMT's said he was out for a minute or two and had a very low blood sugar. That could explain the stumble."

"I'm leaving right now!" Angie could hear Jake. "Nobody can force me to stay. I hate hospitals and if anything happens, it's my responsibility. I might be old, but I'm not senile. I can make my own decisions."

"Jake, what's going on with you? Stop bullying the nurse. She's trying to be sure that you're OK. And please, will you stay for the C-T Scan? I want you for my friend for a lot longer. I don't want to be calling a hearse for you anytime soon!"

Angie said all of this with a warm hug for Jake and a gentle smile. His scowl vanished and he returned her hug with one that was grateful and tight. The normally fierce old man was frightened.

"Geez, Angie, I didn't want them to bother you. You said you were taking the day off."

"Jake, of course they'd call me! That's why you have my card. We take care of each other. I'll stay with you until the scan is done, then we'll get you home. Deal?"

"OK. But I have a date for the weekend. You can bet nothing's going to interfere with that." His blue eyes sparkled at the thought. The nurse with them hid her smile. Angie kept quiet and hoped for the best.

CHAPTER 5
BEN PLANNING

*W*hat kind of VIP client would Angela need to see on her day off? When we were together, she was a Registered Nurse. It sounded as if she has a business now.

After Ben left the atrium where they had spent an hour over coffee, he could still hear Angela's voice, and smell her light spicy-vanilla perfume. Her expressive brown eyes didn't quite hide mixed feelings about him, as hard as she tried to act like a long lost casual friend.

An hour later, jogging along the beachfront, he kept thinking of the morning. *Nobody ever made me feel the way she did. I can't let her go again until she knows everything, even if that's the end of it.*

As he stopped to swab his face, Ben's phone rang. It wasn't the special tone for the boys, and now for Angela as well. Seeing the caller ID jolted him fully into the present.

"Ben, I'm back in town for the weekend and I have seats for tonight's game. Are you by any chance free?"

He usually liked to hear from Ollie. She owned the large, light-filled, oceanfront condo where he was staying until the Cambridge house was ready.

Her motivational seminars were famous around the country, and she was booked solid with prestigious clients. They were glad to give her tickets to almost any show or sporting event, and she could get a table at most top restaurants on the busiest nights.

The invitation brought one problem. Ollie was extremely perceptive when it came to Ben's behavior. They'd been lovers a few years ago. Back then, Ben resented that she put her career before their relationship, and he suspected he wasn't her exclusive partner. The romance faded, although they stayed friends. Lately, he started to think about rekindling things because he was tired of casual dating. She was good at sensing things like that.

But today, he saw Angela. Crazy as it was, that changed the way he felt. He was afraid Ollie would pick up on it. A date with her tonight wasn't the best idea.

"Ollie, I've got a ton of work to finish on a new grant proposal. Its due Monday and I've taken today off completely to do house stuff. I…"

"Ben, stop it. You love football. These are luxury suite tickets. No excuses. Meet me at The Four Seasons at five for drinks. The group has a couple of guest cars going from there."

"Ollie…," But Ben knew he had little choice. He did enjoy Ollie and her celebrity friends. He was using her house too. How could he say no?

It's time to stop thinking about this morning. I don't know if we've even got a chance. So, why do I feel guilty about having a good time with an old friend like Ollie?

Because you know how you feel about seeing Angela, you idiot. That's why.

He thought a hot full-nozzle shower would help to clear his head. But, as he wrapped his six foot-three frame in an oversize bath sheet, Angela was still on his mind.

Against his will, he remembered how they shared one bath sheet in the old days. *She used to towel gently saying, "Ben, don't rub! You want to stay damp-dry so the skin lotion works best." Sometimes she massaged it on. Then we needed a second shower before getting dressed.*

Well, this isn't the old days, and Ollie will expect me to show up looking good and in a party mood. She probably has a suite at the hotel too, just in case. Damn it! Before this morning, I would have enjoyed being seduced.

Ben decided he wouldn't disappoint Ollie, at least by his appearance. A custom-made ocean blue shirt skimmed over his muscled chest. Tailored jeans fit his 36-inch waist perfectly. Even at sixty, he had a body that could hold its own. A soft leather belt, hand-tooled cowboy boots and a tweedy sports jacket completed the outfit.

OK, I'll do. A full-length mirror in the huge closet reflected his casually perfect image. *Ollie'll be pissed when she realizes I'm going home tonight, but she'll be satisfied with the way we look as a couple.*

He dropped his Land Rover with the hotel valet at exactly five minutes before five. Ollie was always on time. He thought it only polite to return the courtesy, since she was gifting him VIP tickets, drinks, and whatever else might present itself.

The bar at the Four Seasons was at the far end of a wide hallway running from the spacious, elegantly marbled lobby. Comfortable upholstered chairs lined the walls. Several people shot admiring looks at Ben walking past them.

Ollie leaned with her back against the bar. She wanted everyone entering the lounge to appreciate her glamorous image and her six foot-one-inch elegance.

Black light-weight wool flair pants paired with a black silk shirt flattered her fuller than average figure. She called attention to her swan neck with a silver and crystal necklace. A narrow silver leather belt lightened the dramatic black outfit. She wore her long brunette hair pulled back into an old-fashioned bun. Diamond studs, large enough to be impressive, softened the severity of the hairdo.

Even though at five feet ten inches in bare feet Ollie had a commanding presence, she always wore heels at least three inches high. Tonight, her soft black leather booties put her close to eye level with Ben.

As usual, there was a crowd surrounding her. "Ben! You're late!" she called across the distance between them. "I was just thinking you might have stood me up."

As he approached her, several of the other men had looks that said, *Yeah, as if that might happen.*

Ollie opened her arms and leaned in for a kiss.

Ben knew she was ready for romance. *Might as well send some signals right away.* He held her tight and gave her an enthusiastic but closed mouth smooch.

She whispered, "Maybe I should look for another suite-mate tonight, Gorgeous?"

Still holding her, "Sweetie, we haven't been suite-mates for a long time," Ben said.

"Yeah but you've been thinking about it lately. I could tell. Has something made you shy?"

He smiled without answering as he untangled himself very gently from her arms.

The *Boston News* photographer got their picture just as they started to break the hug. *My editor is going to love this for the quarterly style edition next month. The two of them look like they're made for a magazine cover.* Ollie gave him their names and her business card. Ben didn't mind. Nobody would give a second thought to him being out on the town with a stunning woman.

She went off to mingle, and he stayed close enough for her to claim him as her date. He quickly saw there was no way Ollie would be lacking attention, so he ordered a Cragganmore single-malt scotch and joined the crowd at the bar.

Just as the group was called to the limos, Ollie took Ben's arm. "Let's enjoy the ride to the stadium. It's been way too long since we've cuddled."

He responded to Ollie's attention and to the scent of her jasmine perfume. It was expensive and sexy, and doing what it was designed to do. They nestled into a soft velvet bench seat at the very back of the limo. She buried her face in his neck and pressed against him, resting one hand lightly on his lap. Her soft fur jacket felt good under his fingers. This time, the kiss they shared was hot and deep. He felt himself getting excited.

"So Ben, are you ready to stop the platonic crap? We used to have a really nice time together, remember?"

"Yeah, we did, and I haven't forgotten anything, but we have company in this buggy. We don't want to start anything we can't finish." He moved her hand.

She looked at him appraisingly. "There wouldn't be anyone causing this sudden shy fellow routine, would there?"

"Look, Ollie, how long will you be in town this time?"

"Just tonight. I'm doing an all-day presentation tomorrow and then going on the road for a month. That's why you're condo-sitting, remember?"

"Sweetheart, I'm really happy to be your adoring date for the game. But let's wait until you're around for a while before we think about anything more serious. I'm kind of old for one night stands."

"Yeah, Ben, I get it. I'm eighteen years younger than you are. I admit I'm not ready to give up the bright lights just yet either, and you insist on strict monogamy in a relationship. So, breakfast together in bed is on hold for a while, I guess."

She moved away a little, pretending to pout. *He'll still be the best looking guy at the stadium, and we'll be the stars of the evening. But there's something going on. And I'm going to find out what.*

"If you want me out of your condo, I can bunk in Cambridge with the boys."

"Like hell you will. I want someone living there that I can trust, and you agreed to do it until the first of November. Please stay."

"You're sure?"

"Yeah, I'm sure. I'm not giving up on us yet, though. Be warned."

26

They settled back on the seats, holding hands lightly. He knew enough not to ignore that warning.

The party from the bar continued in the limo, but Ben knew he'd already had a bit too much to drink. It was going to be soda water for him for the rest of the evening. He was heading home tonight before he was tempted to reconsider being Ollie's suite mate. He couldn't do that while Angela was so much on his mind.

CHAPTER 6
ANGIE EXHALES

Jake still wanted to skip the C-T scan. "Angie, it's been over three hours. I don't have a headache and I'm not sleepy or dizzy. I know damn well where I am, what day it is, and what year it is. Since you're a nurse, you know that means I don't have signs of a brain injury." He was sitting on the side of the stretcher, frowning. "Get this IV out. I'm not waiting any more. I want to pick up a few things for my date tonight."

"OK, Jake, but I'm going to call Eileen if you won't wait for the scan. She needs to watch for things that might indicate some trouble in that thick head of yours." Angie stopped and looked straight at him before continuing. "She'll probably see to it you don't do anything that could raise your heart rate or blood pressure too. Unless, of course, you have a clean bill of health."

Jake's face fell. "Geez, Angie, you're playing dirty. I never thought you'd do that to me."

"Jake, what if she had fallen and passed out for a minute? What would you do?"

"OK, OK. I see your point."

Just then, a young woman from Patient Transport arrived with a wheelchair. "Hi, Mr. Acheson, it's time for your scan. Let me help you into the chair, and we'll hang the IV."

Jake looked incredulous. "Wheelchair? Really? I don't think so, young lady."

"Jake don't start. This kid will get in heaps of trouble if she needs to call her supervisor. Do you want to see her disciplined because she can't do her job?"

"Angie, this is bull..."

"Jake, enough!" Angie whirled toward him. Her voice was low, but sharp as a whiplash. She made it clear the game was getting boring. "Go, or don't go. Ruin your weekend, because Eileen will be very unhappy. Make me crazy with worry. Take a chance on having any kind of life gone forever. But for godssake, quit bitching!"

He roared laughing. "We've been hanging around together too long. That sounded just like me when I'm really pissed."

"Young lady," he turned to the worried looking girl holding the wheelchair, "I will go anywhere you wish to take me." He smiled at her gently. "But I can get myself into the chair if you handle the IV." By the time they got to the radiology unit, the two were friends.

Angie followed, looking relieved.

The scan was finished and no problems were evident. "I won't say I told you so," Jake's tone was sarcastic. Her look told him to quit while he was ahead. The two were in a hurry to go home and get on with their respective evening plans.

Angie waited while he dressed and listened to his discharge instructions. He needed to be careful not to overexert himself and to avoid alcohol and some medications for the next twenty-four hours. He got a list of things that would require an immediate return to the ER. Everything the nurse told him was also in writing. Angie took the papers and told Jake they were going to Eileen. He grudgingly agreed.

On the short ride home, he reminisced about times in the Navy when he was on shore leave and had gotten worse bumps on the head. Angie just smiled without comment.

"So, you're not chatty, Honey. Everything OK? Sorry if I pulled you away from something important."

"Oh, no, Jake. I was just at the mall. But I did run into someone I haven't seen in a long time. It brought back a lot of memories."

Her voice sounded sad and thoughtful. He sensed there was something important about the meeting.

"So, was it an old flame, maybe?" he joked. Angie didn't answer.

"Honey, I didn't mean to pry. You've been great to me today. If you need anyone straightened out or anything, I can still do that."

Angie laughed as she pulled into his driveway. "Jake, maybe I'm the one who needs straightening out. I'm thinking silly thoughts for my age."

"Dan's been gone three years. You deserve a life. Nothing silly about wanting one."

He kissed Angie's cheek, giving her a quick hug. "I'm planning on having a very nice weekend," he told her.

Angie had a date too. She was going to Symphony with Charlie.

Charlie. What is this between Charlie and me? Until recently, we were best buddies.

She remembered the day things changed, and how she never saw it coming.

⇥⇤

Angie loved Tanglewood, with its wide manicured lawns and panoramic views of the Berkshires. The Boston Symphony Orchestra played there during the summer. Before concerts, people picnicked on the grounds, looking over the low rolling hills of Western Massachusetts. Groups scattered under huge old trees, eating meals ranging from sandwiches to gourmet banquets. Some had flowers on portable tables set with crystal and china. The quiet clink of wine glasses under a clear blue sky put everyone in a festive mood.

Charlie had surprised Angie with an elegant array of food, packed in a large wicker basket. When she said she wished they could listen to the music from the private little space they had found, he was glad to stay there instead of taking their seats in the open-sided building.

They drank champagne to the music of Strauss waltzes, and by intermission, Angie was thoroughly relaxed. Charlie had one glass, telling her he had to drive.

I hadn't a second thought when he stretched out on the blanket and took my hand. It was Charlie for godssake. The little kiss on the cheek didn't even tip me off.

He was a lawyer who specialized in divorce. They had met about six months after Dan died. One of his clients needed help with a medical problem, but didn't have a doctor. Charlie knew about Angie's Nurse Concierge business and called her for consultation.

They were impressed with each other, and, when he asked her to have a celebratory dinner after the case was closed, she said yes.

Until that beautiful late August afternoon, he always behaved like a good buddy. He saw other women, making no attempt to hide that his dating included weekends and sleepovers. It was fine with her. She liked Charlie, and they shared an occasional kiss, but there was nothing more between them.

Then, during the second half of the concert, Charlie turned, took her in his arms, and kissed her with passion and sweetness. She was surprised how much she liked it. He was delighted with her response.

"Charlie," she remembered saying, "what's happening here?"

"Angie, we've been hanging out more than a couple of years. You're gorgeous, smart and interesting. I enjoy being with you...a lot."

"I like being with you too, but we've never really dated. We just get together now and then."

"OK. Then I propose we start dating. We could make an evening of it here. There's a great old inn with lots of atmosphere, good food, feather beds..."

"Charlie, that's too far, too fast! Besides, I'm old fashioned about casual sex."

"Gorgeous, trust me. Any sex I have with you will be well planned, not casual."

"You surprised me today. I'd like to date you, but I'm not comfortable sleeping with someone unless it's an exclusive relationship. And it's way too early to think about that."

"It felt as if you liked our kiss, Angie." He still had her in his arms, and started to curve one hand toward her breast. She couldn't deny she enjoyed his touch.

"You know what," she said, pulling away gently, "the concert is almost over, and we're in a public place. Let's start packing up. You are one great kisser Charlie. But I need to take things slowly."

"I am a patient man, Gorgeous. I'm putting you on notice. I didn't hear you say we'd never be together. I can settle for slow."

<hr />

That had been about a month ago. He was still dating others, but they saw each other more and more frequently. She was thinking about telling Charlie on their date tonight it might not be a bad idea to consider having an exclusive relationship.

But I can't do that now. Not after seeing Ben this morning. And I'm scared because I feel that way.

CHAPTER 7

NAN AND ANGIE

The shrill ring awakened Nan. Angie's number glowed on the caller ID.

"What's wrong? Have you been arrested and need bail or something?" She grabbed the phone and went into the bathroom to avoid disturbing her husband.

"I'm OK, I think. Calling to ask you to come over. Now, please."

"Angie, it's still dark, isn't it?" She peeked out the window and saw sun. "OK, so it's sun-up. Wait a sec."

Angie heard her put the phone down, then water running. A minute later, Nan was back. "Are you serious?"

"It's seven-thirty. I've been up since five. I'd come there, but Jim's probably still sleeping."

"Well, yeah," Nan saw her husband already spread out, taking up most of the bed. He was smiling in his sleep. "Lots of people sleep after sun-up on Sunday morning. Unless they haven't been to bed yet."

"Please Nan. Throw on some sweats and just get over here. I have big news."

This has to be something important. She doesn't do things like calling at dawn. "OK. But you'd better give me muffins. Blueberry muffins. And maybe bacon. Give me fifteen minutes."

"That had to be Angie." Jim was awake, but barely. "You'd have taken anybody else's head off. She all right?" He sat up in bed as she slipped gray sweatpants and a hooded shirt on her tall, sleek body. Her long black hair was in a thick braid.

"I think so, Hon. Begged me to come over for breakfast. Sounded like she needed to talk. Go back to sleep. See you in a while. I'll bring a muffin." She kissed him.

"Uh-huh. I'll dream of you." He smiled and returned her kiss. "That minty mouth of yours tastes good."

Nan decided to drive the short distance. She was sitting in her friend's sun-splashed kitchen minutes later, with a cup of fragrant hot coffee in front of her. Fresh blueberry muffins wafted their aroma from the oven. She didn't want to wait another minute to find out what was going on. "So, you dragged me out of a very comfy bed at dawn to hear some news. Stop puttering and tell me, dammit!"

Angie was busy piling crisp bacon onto a serving plate. "You said I had to give you breakfast. I'm fixing exactly what you ordered."

"Stop being a pain in the ass."

As she turned and put the hot muffins, along with sweet butter, in a basket on the table Angie said, "I saw Ben."

Nan's eyes widened and her mouth opened in surprise. She curbed her explosive reaction. Without interrupting, she listened, eating bits of muffin and bacon, until Angie finished her story. Then she answered, almost in disbelief.

"You ran into Ben? Yesterday? That rotten British bastard Ben? And you actually talked to him instead of calling the cops and reporting him for emotional abuse? There shouldn't be a statute of limitations on that. It's like murder!"

She watched her friend with concern and curiosity. Angie was smiling and her eyes glowed.

Nan would never forget the phone call from her twenty-four years ago. There was just a whimper at first, like the sound from an injured animal. She gulped out the story between sobs, while Nan made soothing sounds. She stayed with Angie for three days, listening, forcing her to eat and drink enough to stay alive, and holding her while she cried and howled between bouts of restless sleep.

For a year after, Angie's life was work, the gym, and not much else. She adopted a noisy black and white cat for company. Feeding and petting Bingo got her out of bed on the bad mornings.

Now, over two decades later, Ben was back. "Tell me, what's going on in your head?"

"Nan, I don't know. I'm torn. I nearly died when he left. In fact, a part of me did die. I was never able to be that open again with anybody. I loved Dan. It was a good marriage, but I always held a little of myself in reserve, like an emergency kit in case something went wrong."

"And how did you feel seeing Ben again?"

"As if I found something wonderful that I thought was lost forever."

Nan was quiet.

"I had to leave because I was paged, but he made sure to give me his phone number. He said the ball was in my court, but I know he really wants to get together again."

"And you, do you want to? He might take off again and leave you miserable, you know."

"Nan, I have to at least know what happened. He said he's single now, but he has two boys living in Cambridge, starting grad school."

"OK. That would mean they were born around the time he left."

"Don't you think I realize that?" Angie snapped. Then she immediately took Nan's hand across the table. "I'm sorry. I have no right to speak to you so nastily. I know you're just trying to help me sort this out. Am I crazy?"

"Angie, it doesn't matter what I think. You've got to do what feels right. There's no perfect solution. If you let him back into your life, you can get terribly hurt. If you don't, you'll always wonder. Just be careful. Of course, there's Charlie in the wings. Things are moving along with him as I remember."

Angie munched on bacon and poured them more coffee. "Oh yes, Charlie. The great kisser Charlie who's started to include boob massages with his hugs? The man who says he's ready to give up his other ladies for me. That Charlie?"

Nan smiled. "So, what happened?"

"We had a date last night for the symphony. There was a benefit reception after, and when I came back from the ladies' room, Liliana Barker was sitting in my seat. She looked like a movie star in a painted-on silver dress, slit to her waist and up to her butt. Worst part was, it looked great on her."

"Liliana? Isn't she the real estate lady who sells most of Rock Harbor and Plover Cove?" Nan slipped another piece of crisp bacon onto her plate. "Well, it was a benefit. Maybe they're just business acquaintances."

"Nan," she leaned toward her friend, "she was hammered. When I came back she said, 'Angie! Are you a friend of Charlie's? We were just talking about our cruise to the Caribbean next week.' For godssake, she even said they'd only need carry-ons because the ship had a clothing optional pool and deck area!"

Nan couldn't keep a straight face. "Well, he's probably just honoring his prior commitments before coming to you totally free."

"Yeah, well, I don't think Charlie's going to be totally free any time soon!"

"So what did you say?"

"He looked so flustered, I had a fit of laughing, and I couldn't say much. She gave him an X-rated kiss, where one of her hands was hidden between them for a minute, and he blushed! He got red, honestly!"

"I'd have paid admission to see that act," Nan was laughing out loud. "It must've been a helluva ride home for you two."

"Not really. I was relieved not to need an excuse to cool things. We stopped for a drink at the Plover Cove Tavern. I think he knew he wasn't going to be invited in when we got here. He apologized all over the place, said that some folks were harder to untangle from than others. I told him to forget it, these things take time. I did remind him, though, that I haven't changed my mind about sharing lovers with other women."

"Just last week you were open to trying a serious relationship with Charlie. Let's see, can I guess what might have changed your mind so fast?" Nan lifted a perfectly groomed eyebrow.

"Before you say it, yes, my head was still with Ben. I can't stop thinking about him."

"Well, you have his phone number. People text these days. Email is so old." Nan continued. "We're the sisters we never had, Angie. I will listen, I will not judge, and I will be nice to that bastard if that's what you want, unless he hurts you again. Then I will not be nice to him. In fact, I will be very nasty."

Standing, she said, "I'm taking a muffin for Jim. It's a good thing he's the kind of husband who understands my bolting from the house at dawn. Come to the club this afternoon. It's the first weekend off you've had in a while."

As Nan was leaving, a deliveryman with a huge vase full of pink and white roses was about to ring the bell. "Hey, Angie," she called, "Someone's here with half a florist shop!"

"There must be at least two dozen roses here, Nan! Oh Gawd! They're from Charlie."

"So what's the card say?"

"Angie, I am an ass, but a recovering one. Don't give up on me. Love, C."

"OK then, Looks like Charlie isn't out of the running after all. This ought to be interesting, Angie." She left, shaking her head and chuckling.

Angie put the beautiful bouquet on the coffee table in her living room, then emailed Charlie.

"Yes, you are an ass, but you're a nice one. Thanks for the lovely posies. There's lots of time for recovery."

She signed it "your dear friend" just to let him know she wasn't letting him off the hook.

Then she went to get the large purse she had carried at the mall. Ben's card was in her wallet. It was thick linen

39

and, in embossed letters, said Benjamin Whitcomb, without a title. There were two printed phone numbers, with emails, for London, England and Naples, Florida. Then, there was the handwritten number and an email he had given her. *There's no way I'm contacting him for at least a couple of days. I have plenty to keep myself busy. I'll go to the Sunday cocktail thing at the yacht club. I have three books on my to-read list. I have paperwork to finish. Besides, a weekday get together isn't as big a deal as a weekend one. Maybe we can have coffee again. Breakfast before work is good too. That way there's no candlelight or wine and it can't last too long.*

Angie realized without any doubt. She had decided to see Ben again.

CHAPTER 8
BEN'S MORNING AFTER

S unlight flooded the bedroom by the time Ben awakened on Sunday morning. It was late for him, at seven-thirty. He vaguely realized something good had happened the day before, but his foggy mind couldn't focus on details yet. A mild headache nudged memories of a little too much Scotch, along with Ollie's nearly successful try to rekindle their love affair, but there was something else.

Then the reason he was waking up alone, without Ollie's ample, delicious body nestled next to him, popped into his mind.

Angela! He ran into her, well, she actually ran into him, yesterday. *With her so fresh in my mind, I couldn't be with another woman last night.*

He got out of bed slowly, seriously considering skipping his morning run. However, when Ben splashed water on his face, routine took over. In minutes, he was out the door and setting a pace along the walk bordering the sandy beach. It was an autumn ocean now, blowing breezes with a tinge of the chill to come. Blue wavelets were darker than the summer swells.

I told Angela the ball is in her court to get in touch with me. I'll wait, but only for another day or two. She did give me her email. Copying her home address might have been a little sneaky, but the envelope was in plain sight on the table. It'll make it easier to get her phone number if I need it. I can't believe how good it felt to see her.

Salty gusts banished the headache and his body kicked into gear. Ben was running slowly, enjoying the brisk air. A couple of the guys at last night's party had suggested an afternoon sail out of Rock Harbor. He accepted the invitation and looked forward to being on the water. They mentioned going to a cocktail party at one of the yacht clubs after the sail.

That'd be a good way to make some connections up here. If the boys stay in the area, I may visit more often. Then of course, Angela lives in the next town. Daft thinking, Mate. Way too early in the game to be considering that.

Ben's message ping was sounding when he got back to the condo. *I am off-kilter this morning! I never forget my phone. Who's looking for me before nine on a Sunday? Wouldn't put it past Ollie. That woman is on a mission.*

The text was from Pete, one of his twin sons.

Hey, dunk, u ok? Wazzup? Call.

It made Ben smile. The boys had been with him since they were a year old, and he legally adopted them within months. He wanted them to realize they were born to loving parents, so he never called himself their father. As they learned to talk, he became Unk.

When they asked why Ben wasn't their Dad, he carefully told them about the accident that took their parents, his sister and her husband. After some serious discussions, the boys decided he was really their dad-uncle, but that was too long. Dunk was the compromise for five year olds, and Ben was fine with it. The name stuck.

He called Pete's cell. "Hi. Always good to hear from you, but why the worry?"

"You sure you're OK, Dunk? Ollie said she was worried."

"Ollie." Ben kept the anger out of his voice.

"Yeah. She called this morning with a last minute invitation to brunch for Ryan, me, and whomever we want to bring. Mentioned you seemed off your feed last night, so she didn't ask you. Said we could though."

"Nope, I'm great. That was nice of Ollie. Didn't know you kept in touch. Are you and Ryan going?"

Ben could feel his temple pulse. He was furious. Worrying the boys was way over the line. Ollie knew those rules. She was either tipsy on early morning mimosas or wildly curious.

"No, can't. He has a, well, commitment this morning, and I have study group."

Ben chuckled at that. "I'll bet Ryan's commitment is a lovely lady."

The boys met Ollie several years ago when she and Ben were a little more than friends. She was always very good with them, and they liked her. It was nice of her to keep in touch. But this was a dirty trick.

"Can the two of you manage a meal sometime this week if I come to Cambridge?"

"I'll set it up with Ryan, Dunk. When?"

"Except for tomorrow, whenever you can do it."

"OK. Sure everything is good? Ollie really was concerned."

"Everything is fine, Pete. I'll touch base with Ollie."

"Fine. I'll text you when I get hold of Ryan. He'll probably surface for air by this afternoon."

Ben was still fuming when he hung up. *Hell! I need to cool down before I talk to Ollie. She has no scruples when it comes to getting what she wants. She's not worried about me, just aggravated that I didn't want to spend the night. Fishing to know if there's something she doesn't know about. Surprising she involved the boys though. They've always been off-limits. A text will do for now.*

He thought for a few minutes before sending the message.

U went way over line. Stop. Now. U have?? ask me. Do again, we R finished for good.

A quick shower, made him remember mornings with Angela again. He shook himself damp-dry like a wet dog, finished with a brisk towel rub and slipped into old sweat pants and a soft tee. Barefoot, he went to the kitchen, poured himself a big cup of coffee and ate whole grain toast with peanut butter before settling at the desk.

Have to get the funding proposal finished for tomorrow. That nonprofit needs money and I can't use what they gave me without some additions and polishing.

Ben had the luxury of working only on projects he enjoyed. As a young stockbroker in Boston, he earned enough money to live very nicely. Unlike many of his peers, he didn't blow it on drugs, booze, and expensive women. Ben invested with a good sense of what would benefit clients. His customer list grew by referrals.

The Young Genius, people called him. He succeeded because he worked sixteen-hour days studying the market, contacting new leads and learning from experienced and successful brokers.

"For chrissake, Ben, loosen up a little," was something he often heard from the other young men in the office. Sometimes he would join them for drinks after work, but, more often than not, he'd leave early. Even without a lot of partying together, people liked him.

One thing he made time for was volunteering for charities. He served on two boards and spent Saturday afternoons playing basketball with kids who lived in shelters.

Otherwise, except for work functions, Ben didn't spend time playing. He met Angela when he was thirty-five, and fell in love almost immediately. They were happy from the start, delighted to have found each other. Of course, everything changed when he cut her off so brutally. But, as he thought to himself thousands of times before, *Right or wrong, back then, I couldn't see another choice.*

Ben was already wealthy when he gained control of a large inheritance. His grandfather was an American contractor who died a very rich man when Ben was fifteen. They were always close. He loved the way the old man talked to him as if he were the most important person in the world. It took some of the sadness away when Ben was seven and his father died.

His grandfather never trusted the man Ben's mother married two years later. The will stipulated that only Ben and his sister could get their inheritance unless they died or were otherwise unable to manage it. In that case, a trusted set of advisors, not their stepfather or mother, would control it. When he did get the money at forty years old, he multiplied it buying London real estate before the boom. He was the trustee for his sister's share, which the boys would get.

He made another fortune selling to buyers willing to pay huge sums when real estate became hot. At the same time, Ben continued to receive impressive commissions as a successful investment counselor.

Although now he was rich enough to do whatever he liked, he continued to work hard as an unpaid consultant for non-profit organizations. Ben also earned healthy fees for matching companies who were looking for partners or funds. Most of that money went to worthy causes. His business kept him active and involved with interesting, smart people.

Ben ignored three calls from Ollie. He never bothered to respond to her texts pleading:

OMG let me at least explain.

CHAPTER 9
ANGIE AND BEN AGAIN

Angie looked forward to spending a few hours without thinking about work, Ben, or anything but having some cold white wine and catching up with friends. *I'm unavailable until tomorrow morning for everybody, except Jake of course, but he's with Eileen, so no worries. I can't remember the last time I took myself off the grid like this.*

The harbor view looked like a giant seascape with sapphire water and foamy wavelets as she walked into the open, sunny room. Ocean air on the first day of October carried salty breezes from the terrace.

"Hey, Angie, you really made it!" Nan's husband, Jim, motioned her over to a merry group.

"My god, you did take the day off. I can't remember the last time you wore a dress. That yellow looks gorgeous. Trying to impress someone?" It was Nan, delighted that her friend had joined them and seemed ready to have fun. "Someone get this woman a Pinot Grigio with ice. She needs to catch up."

People mingled and flowed, creating a pretty swirl of tanned folks dressed in casually elegant nautical or pastel colored outfits. Some were just back from late sailing, others from a last dip in the ocean or pool. Laughter, the tinkling of ice cubes, and an occasional loud exclamation punctuated the conversations. There were a few people, heads together, sharing a quiet story.

I'll bet some interesting news is being passed along in those little groups. It's been too long since I've been part of this crowd.

"Angie, you look lovely!" It was Liliana, the woman who had staked her claim on Charlie the evening before.

"Liliana. Nice to see you again."

"I'm sure, Dear. Look, I had a touch more to drink than I usually do last night. Hope I wasn't, well, inappropriate, in any way. It's just that Charlie and I are really good friends, and I didn't expect to see him…thought he was out of town, fishing, or something equally boring."

"Not at all, Liliana. Don't give it a second thought."

"Hadn't intended to, but he called this morning. Said I had been obnoxious and to cool it. Enjoy the afternoon." She scanned the room and abruptly turned away.

Angie noticed that the woman wore an expertly fitted navy blue silk tank over white raw silk slacks. *How the hell does she walk in those sandals? They've got to have three-inch heels.* She was conscious of her own ballet flats and slightly fitted A-line linen dress. *Well, at least it's not my summer uniform… khakis, some kind of shirt and a linen blazer.*

"Hey, Angie, what's going on?" Jeannie and Bob Craigan, the owners of Rock Harbor Posies, were heading toward her. Bob's voice lowered to nearly a whisper. "Did you like the roses? Charlie got me up this morning, way too early for a Sunday. Said it was an emergency and to send you as many roses as I could find. Everything OK?"

Everybody knew most everybody else in Rock Harbor, so Angie wasn't surprised that Charlie's urgent order generated some curiosity. Bob's wife rescued her.

"I keep reminding Bob that florists are bound by confidentiality about the same as lawyers and clergy. Sometimes he's just too nosey, Angie. But you can be sure he won't mention this to anyone else. Will you, Sweetie?" Jeannie gave her husband a swift poke to his ribs and a steely look.

Ambling over, Charlie gently took Angie's half-finished glass from her hand and replaced it with another. "Hope you're all having a great time. Here's a fresh wine, Angie. That one's probably watery now." It was exactly as she liked it, in a large bowl glass with lots of ice. She noticed that his hand lingered on hers.

His madras slacks, although retro, fitted the oceanfront scene to a tee. The time he spent at the gym was obvious the way the bright yellow polo draped across his chest.

He's as good looking as Ben.

Angie surprised herself with the thought. The purpose of this afternoon was to forget Ben and have fun. She gave Charlie a genuinely happy smile. "You can be a very thoughtful fellow when you try. Maybe there's hope yet."

Jeannie knew when to exit. "Nice to see you both. Come on, Bob, let's get a drink. We're monopolizing Angie." She literally pulled her curious husband away.

"Geez, Hon," he remarked, "I think old Charlie is hooked this time." She smiled. "Maybe, Sweetie, but Angie is a catch. There might be some competition."

"What d'ya mean?"

"I just have a feeling."

"I am really embarrassed about last night." Charlie had to clear his throat before and after he said that. He scanned Angie's face intently, waiting for a reaction.

"Charlie, we're only just thinking about getting more serious. No harm done yet. We'll go slowly. I'm just old fashioned about sex. I don't do casual hook-ups…didn't when everybody else did. Love to kiss though. Love getting flowers too. We're good."

They were interrupted by the sound of loud welcomes near the door.

"Hey, where'd you guys come from?" The group sounded glad to see whoever it was.

"Wanted to try a sail around Rock Harbor for a change. Picked up these sorry wrecks from the game last night." A trio of tall men returned the friendly greetings. The shortest, who was at least six feet, spoke first. "Borrowed a boat from a friend for a couple of hours this afternoon and decided to crash the party. Who'll buy us a drink?"

Angie was stunned. There, Ben stood with the newcomers. He was the tallest of the three, his gray hair tousled from the wind, looking like he should be in a sailing poster.

"Excuse me Charlie. I'll be back in a sec."

Nan seldom missed a trick. She saw Angie's face change from carefree to surprised, then confused, as she abruptly left Charlie for the ladies' lounge.

"That fellow looks enough like Ben to be his twin, doesn't he?" Jim asked. Without answering, Nan got up and made a beeline to the lounge. She found Angie slumped on a couch, staring at her half-empty wine glass.

"What the hell am I going to do Nan?"

"We probably know that already." Hugging her friend, she added, "Let the games begin."

CHAPTER 10
THE GAMES BEGIN

When Angie rejoined the party, Charlie motioned her over to a crowd surrounding the recent arrivals. With an arm around her waist, he told her that one of them was Kevin Ruskin, an excellent client. He added there was no need for him to crash any parties because he had reciprocal privileges at almost every yacht club on the East Coast. The other two were his guests.

"Kevin, meet a friend of mine, Angie Martin-Wilson. Angie, say hello to Kevin and friends."

"Oh, my pleasure," the man greeted her warmly. "Charlie always knows the prettiest women! Angie, Charlie, these gents are Rick Thompson and Ben Whitcomb."

Angie's smile was both impish and dazzling as she faced the two men and offered her hand.

"Hello, Rick."

"Nice to see you so soon again," she greeted Ben.

"Oh lord, how do you two know each other?" Kevin asked Ben.

Charlie was all ears. He was such a good lawyer because he read people well, and there was something here. Ben's smile lit up his face. Angie glowed with a slight flush. He could feel her body tighten a bit under his encircling arm.

"Ben and I knew each other a lot of years ago. I ran into him yesterday at a shopping mall. We had a chance to catch up a little. Today is a pleasant surprise."

"Isn't it though?"

Ben's warm response annoyed Charlie. "Well, you'll all want to grab a drink after that sail. We'll catch you later." He guided Angie away.

"Charlie! You were barely polite. And we're not a "we" yet. Remember?"

Liliana was heading toward the group around Kevin and his friends. She managed to join the laughing crowd, and edged closer to Ben.

After some casual conversation, he went to the bar, ordered, handed Liliana a cosmo, then headed out on the deck alone. He seemed to be taking a few pictures with his phone.

This is nuts. I want to see him again. Angie drifted to the deck and leaned on the white rail next to Ben. The late flowers wafted their perfume. "So. Here we are. Coincidence, or something else?" It was a teasing comment.

"Don't know. But I'm very happy to see you." His hazel eyes caught hers in a look that didn't waver.

She leaned a bit closer. "Ben, do you have time to grab a late breakfast Tuesday? If you want to, of course."

His smile widened. "Sure. That would be lovely, Angela. You have all my numbers. Let me know where and when."

"OK. There's a little Italian place on Bogart Street in Plover Cove. Their omelets are delicious."

"Vianni's? I've seen it."

"How about ten? I have an early morning presentation, but I'll be free by then."

Vianni's is a local spot. Not many people outside of Rock Harbor and Plover Cove know about it. He must be staying somewhere close by. I'd love to know exactly where, but no way am I going to ask. It's really none of my business. At least, not yet. Maybe never.

Jim, Nan, and Charlie joined them. "Long time, no see, Ben." Jim greeted him warmly.

"That's for sure," Nan commented. Her smile was tight, and her voice might have had a little edge to those who knew her well.

Charlie sensed that something was in the air besides salt and the scent of late geraniums.

Liliana joined them all, with her laser-blue eyes fixed on Ben.

"It's been a long and lovely afternoon, but I've got some prep to do for work tomorrow." Angie kissed Charlie's cheek and hugged Nan and Jim goodbye. She waved at Liliana.

Ben grasped her hand as she turned to leave. "It was great to see you again today, Angela." She smiled without commenting.

"See you all later."

She didn't pull away from this guy when he caught her hand. She's usually not touchy-feely with strangers. Charlie decided he'd find out more about Ben Whitcomb.

She started her car quickly. *Charlie's going to want to talk about how I know Ben, and I'm not ready for that discussion. He's probably on his way to catch me before I leave.* She pulled out of the lot just as he rounded the corner on foot.

After Angie left, Ben and Jim sat at a back table on the terrace, away from the crowd, both drinking MacCallan 15 year old Scotch. "My treat, Ben, as a welcome back token."

"She doesn't know why I left yet, Jim. I've no idea how she'll react. Did you tell Nan?"

Jim answered softly. "No. It's one of the few secrets I've never shared with her. She'd have been in an awful position. They're closer than sisters. How could I expect her to keep something like that from Angie? I'll admit, I had to be really on guard. Nan loves to hear the down and dirty about those London meetings."

"I put you in a tough spot by telling you, then swearing you to secrecy. I can feel Nan's fury still simmering even after twenty-four years."

"Hey, I almost punched you out that day we ran into each other on Fleet Street. I ripped you up and down and called you the lowest son-of-a-bitch in creation. I swear you dragged me into the Cheshire Cheese pub to keep me from killing you on the spot."

Ben chuckled. "Yeah, you were pretty pissed. You'd been my best friend for a long time, and I just couldn't stand that going south as well as everything else I'd left behind. That's why I told you everything."

"To this day, I think Angie'd have been OK with not being your whole life for a while, but that wasn't my call. Nan's been mildly pissed at me for not hating you as much as she has all these years. She'd throw me out on my ass if she ever even thought I knew anything she didn't."

Ben leaned a little closer across the table. "Jim, I'd die before I'd tell her...or Angela."

"Hey, Ben, you wouldn't have a choice. I'd kill you myself if you told either of them about our conversation." Jim's tone was serious. "What was it, about twenty years ago?"

"Yeah. Wish I'd have kept in touch." Ben dropped his eyes, sighed, then straightened in his chair.

"So then, Mate, I have to be on my way. Need to be up at dawn tomorrow. I'm due at a D.C. ten AM meeting to help a kids' nonprofit wring some funding out of tight-fisted bureaucrats. You know what Logan and Regan will be like on a Monday morning. I'm flying commercial, not corporate."

"OK Ben." They man-hugged each other. "It's great to have you back. When're you seeing Angie again?"

"How do you know I am?"

"I'm not a dumb bastard. That's how." Jim cuffed Ben's arm lightly.

"Tuesday. She invited me to a late breakfast at Vianni's. I pray she'll hear me out and at least understand. Maybe even consider us seeing each other again."

Jim saw his wife approaching.

"There's Nan, scanning the area for me. She'll want to hear about every word. I'll pretend I had too much booze. Let her blame you for my condition. What the hell, you're on her shit list anyway. Oh, by the way, I think you've got a shot, even with the competition."

As he slipped down the back stairs, before Nan reached them, Ben thought about the competition. The guy with his arm around Angie. He remembered the name, *Charlie*.

Ben had felt a little pang as he watched the ruggedly handsome man spirit Angela away from Kevin's group as quickly as he could and still be reasonably courteous.

"He's one of the sharpest divorce lawyers on the East Coast," Kevin, his sailing host, had said. "Charlie saved me a fortune with both wives, and finally convinced me to do an uncrackable pre-nup with this one. I think she's going to be around for the full show though. Helps that she's rich enough not to worry about my wad. Made me sign a pre-nup too. Love that girl!"

Charlie spotted our quick hand grasp when she left. He didn't look happy. I'm thinking he's not going to welcome competition for Angela's attention.

CHAPTER 11
BACK TO WORK

Ben

A car picked Ben up at five-thirty Monday morning. He'd slept five hours after the party.

The Washington meetings were long, but successful. Thanks to his proposal and some connections he had, the kids' charity got the five hundred thousand dollar grant.

In D.C., there were a couple of highly placed folks who wanted some free advice and asked him to dinner. They went on to a very private club after, where good Scotch and useful gossip flowed freely. Ben drank little, and listened carefully.

He was back in Plover Cove at midnight.

Thoughts about Angela and what he had to tell her kept him awake.

I'm more nervous about seeing her than I've ever been for a meeting with millions of dollars at stake.

Angie

Monday morning, Angie couldn't stop thinking about the club party. *Charlie didn't like me responding to Ben. Was I that obvious? Probably. The only reason I asked him to breakfast was to get answers. Then it'll be finished and I can get back to my life.* There was a nagging taunt deep in her mind. *You really think so?* She thought about the email she sent after finishing her work last night.

"Looking forward to Tuesday, A."

It was ridiculous how it pleased her to discover he had sent one earlier.

"Thanks for the invitation, Angela. Wonderful seeing you today. Ben"

I've survived for twenty-four years without him or knowing what happened. Why dig up old wounds? Maybe I should cancel breakfast tomorrow. That idea made her sad enough to stop daydreaming and take a shower.

She knew the day ahead was busy enough to make her forget Ben, Charlie, and whatever drama might be in the future.

Her Nurse Concierge business helped people to find the best health care services for their situation. Angie and her staff made sure their clients knew what choices were available and had the information they needed to make decisions. When necessary, a staff member would go to appointments, arrange care at home, and do other things to keep clients as informed, safe, and comfortable as possible.

As she dressed, Angie thought about her client schedule for the day. Two daughters and a son were concerned about their ninety-year-old parents. They wanted them to move to Assisted Living. The parents were determined to stay put in the home where they'd lived for sixty-five years.

The kids thought the parents were incapable of making good decisions. The parents, on the other hand, had consulted their attorney and were threatening to remove the children as their trustees unless they stopped pushing. The family wanted somebody to help sort through available choices for a safe compromise. Angie had asked several members of her team to join the meeting.

Eating a breakfast of rye toast with peanut butter, she had her second client in mind. He was unhappy with his primary care physician. "The dang doctor never explains my diagnosis or why he wants me to take medicines. I ask, but he brushes me off. It'd be hard to start with another doc, even if I could find one." Angie needed to hear more.

She was planning to drop in on two more clients in the hospital. One of her most important services was to be sure any help and equipment they might need were in place for clients when they got home, and that prescriptions were accurate and ready for pickup or delivery.

Angie's business started by chance when she helped a friend who didn't understand how to get a second opinion about surgery. That resulted in referrals from other people who were confused about what their insurance would cover for bills. Finally, one of her satisfied clients told her to start charging for her time and expertise.

Now Angie had a full team available for clients. Her Licensed Clinical Social Worker, RN's, consulting Elder Law Attorney and Physician Advisor worked well together. They had become friends as well as colleagues.

Each one had urged Angie to cut back a bit on working personally with clients. She managed the business and did most of the marketing and speaking engagements.

"You need to have a life besides work, Angie. You pull more than your share."

She had heard those comments frequently. The group was delighted when she took nearly all of the last weekend off.

Of course, everybody knew Jake was very special. That's why the on-call RN notified her about his Emergency Room visit on what was supposed to be her Saturday off.

Angie admitted to herself that she hid behind her career sometimes.

Dan used to get a little impatient about the time I spent on work. In the last two years, he seemed preoccupied anyway. But our marriage was fine, even if the fire had waned a bit. He may have felt lousy frequently, not that he said much. He kept a lot of things to himself.

Now that I think of it, Ben was a little jealous any time I worked extra hours. We skirmished about it if he had to change plans when I covered for an unexpected sick call or emergency. I wonder if he's still that way?

As she sat in her mildly messy, plant-filled office, Angie's inner thoughts wouldn't quit. *I feel useful when I work. It fills the time. I don't need to worry about anything but taking care of my clients. I don't think of growing old alone. Having Charlie around to date a little is fine. He respects what I do and he doesn't give me a hard time about the occasional cancellation.*

Thinking about Charlie lightened her mood and she laughed. *Of course he doesn't! If I'm busy, he has his other ladies. He really is a scoundrel. But I do like him. Maybe it could still work. Or maybe not. He'd do fine either way.*

"But, what about me?" She asked herself that question out loud.

Her office manager tapped lightly on the doorframe, a porcelain mug of coffee in her hand.

"Angie, the Filmores are in the conference room. Mom and Pop are on one side of the table and the three kids are on the other. I've set them up with coffee and tea. Here's yours...you'll probably need it."

"OK, Helen, I'm on my way." A last look in her mirror reflected an attractive woman, wearing light make-up, dressed in a crisp white shirt under a summer weight forest green jacket. Her 8mm pearl studs and the gold chain at her neck softened the professional look just enough. Angie always wore khaki slacks in the summer with flat dressy shoes. She never knew what she might need to carry or when a client wanted to take a walk to discuss things.

As she neared the door, she heard raised voices. There was no more time for introspection.

After an hour, The Filmores were at the truce stage. They learned that there were ways for Mr. And Mrs. to remain at home, and still be safe. They could control their own lives. Angie would have specific steps for them to consider at the next meeting.

The next appointment was less complex. Mr. Reynolds was a smart and reasonable man. His physician of forty years had considered patients as colleagues with valuable input for their own treatment. According to Mr. Reynolds, the new doctor changed a lot of meds that had worked well, and expected patients to accept his treatment and advice without question or compromise.

"Well, how about I go to the next appointment with you? You can tell the doctor that you want me to hear what's going on to be sure you don't miss anything."

Mr. Reynolds looked doubtful. "OK, but can you help me find someone else if this doesn't work out?"

"Yes, I can, but it may take time to get you into a new practice. So you don't want to burn bridges right away. Let's be optimistic for the moment, OK?"

She telephoned Mr. Reynolds' Physician's Practice Manager and had the release of information forms faxed over immediately. He would have to sign them before the office could provide any details about his medical issues.

After a quick and late lunch, Angie visited the hospital. Everything was in place for her clients to go home the following day. She was out of there in an hour.

Her phone pinged with a text. It was Nan.

Hey, Angie, How bout the gym in an hr&burger&wine? Jim's wrkng.

She answered,

Y not. C U.

By five-thirty, they were greeting each other with hugs. The two women worked out at least three times a week, and enjoyed a friendly competition when they could. They started with stretching and progressed to cardio.

After forty-five minutes, they were ready to quit.

"I really hate this crap," Nan muttered from the elliptical. She was perspiring heavily.

"Treadmill's easier, but still not my first choice after work." Angie mopped her face and started a cool down.

Nan grinned suggestively. "And your first choice for calorie burning exercise after work would be...?"

"Kickboxing with you as a target!"

"Yeah. Wouldn't oil wrestling with a very tall Brit be more fun?"

Angie laughed in spite of herself. "Let's get some wine. It's still warm enough to sit outside, so we don't even need to shower."

They sat on a lighted patio, each drinking a white wine to the sound of soft Latin music. After rehashing the party the day before, Angie said, "I'm meeting him for breakfast tomorrow."

Nan hailed the waiter. "Two more wines and a plate of Nachos, please."

"We've already had one wine, and *Nachos* for goddsake? What happened to burgers without the buns?"

"Listen, I'm going to need alcohol and comfort food for this story. And since you're the reason I need the sedative effect of fat and carbs, you have to share the calories." She settled back in her seat.

Angie laughed, then told Nan about the emails and that Ben knew Vianni's. "I have to see him, Nan. Just to fix the way we ended. I know I shouldn't consider anything more. Still…" She looked away.

Her friend picked up a nacho dripping with cheese and smiled. "I saw you yesterday, on the terrace with him before we came out there. And, much as I hate to say it, I could see the heat waves between you two. You're both lousy fakers. Yeah, you do have to see him, and I think for more than just making peace. You don't want to spend the rest of your life wondering, Hon."

With Nan's blessing, Angie slept soundly. She dreamed about the email Ben sent just before she went to bed.

"Vianni's at 10. I'll be waiting."

CHAPTER 12

ANTICIPATION

*W*onder *what breakfast will bring between Angela and me?*
Was Ben's first thought when he awakened at seven
AM. He got up and into his running gear. *Half an hour of a
slow run will calm the nerves.* His text signal pinged twice as
he brushed his teeth.

The first was from Pete.

*Dunk, Can U meet me & R. for early dinner in Cambridge?
Fire Phoenix in Kendall sq. at 6? Great Chinese.*

Ben answered immediately.

C U there. D.

*It'll give me a chance to see how the top floor reno is going.
Ollie'll be home in three weeks and there's no way I can stay in the
condo if she's here. Too bad. I like it on the North Shore.*

*Maybe I could rent a little place somewhere close. We'll see how
things go today.*

He hadn't seen the boys for a while and looked forward
to listening to whatever they wanted to share. Ben did his
best raising his adopted sons to become the kind of men
he'd want for friends.

He was closely involved in their lives when they were children, and backed off gradually as they grew up. He always knew what was going on with them, but Ben kept interference at a minimum.

It seemed to pay off. The young men were smart, with a sense of purpose. They were pleasant and humorous with good street sense and respect for others. They made and kept friends and were welcomed anywhere they wanted to go.

The women they dated were all attractive in some way, and the ones he met seemed nice. Other than teaching them responsible sex and general respect for women, he didn't pry. He did tell them that if they got anyone pregnant, they would take excellent care of mother and child for life and any children would have the family name.

Ben knew that Julia, nanny-turned-stepmother, contributed to their successful upbringing as much as he did. After a mutually friendly divorce, the boys continued to adore her.

Ryan and Pete had no idea about the extent of their wealth. Ben was the trustee of the inheritance each would get at thirty. He was generous enough with an allowance so they could do anything they reasonably wanted to, but they had to ask for extras. He funded a small garage start-up that had something to do with robots. Pete was the tech guy and Ryan handled the business. So far, they seemed to be having fun.

The second text was from Ollie.

OK. uv been mad for 2 d. Am very sorry. Miss U. Dinner in NY Sat? my treat.XX

He needed to think about a response.

Too much on my mind. I'll deal with that later. Ben took a gulp of coffee and started his run.

⊷┼┽⊶

Like Ben, Angie was awake before the alarm on the day of their breakfast.

Five minutes after she turned on the kitchen light at six, her phone rang. She already knew who it was. Jake didn't believe in texts.

"Hey, Honey, you're up early."

"Hi Jake. Couldn't sleep, so decided to take time for an extra cup of coffee. You OK?"

"Sure am. Haven't seen you for a couple of days. But I know everything's OK with you, maybe better than that, according to the folks at Ginger's."

"Geez, Jake, I don't know why anyone bothers with newspapers or computers when news spreads like wildfire at that breakfast place." She paused. "So what'd you hear? No, first tell me how things went over the weekend with Eileen."

"I was fine, and still am. Eileen says thank you for taking care of me, and wants to know if you can have dinner with us tonight. I got a lot of indoor exercise this weekend with no problems. We walked a little too." Angie could hear the smile in his voice.

"Great. So, what's the news from Ginger's?" She knew some of the yacht club crowd went there for breakfast. Charlie often stopped in too.

"C'mon over for a cup of coffee and I'll tell you."

"Jake, I have to get to work!"

67

"OK, so the news from Ginger's can wait."

"All right. But just for a few minutes, and I'm in PJs and a bathrobe."

"I'm pouring your cup. Already got your paper, it's tucked in your screen door."

She put on sweats over the oversized tee and ancient gym shorts she slept in, slipped on flip-flops and crossed the street to Jake's. Angie was glad to have someone to talk to for the extra time she had.

"OK Jake, tell me!" She was sitting in his sunroom on a rocker.

"What, no 'nice to see you,' or anything?" Jake settled himself on the other side of the white wicker table.

"JAKE!"

"OK, OK. Charlie stopped by early yesterday wanting to know if anybody had heard of Ben Whitcomb, an Englishman who was at the Club party on Sunday, a friend of Kevin's. One guy remembered the name from when he worked in Boston. Said Whitcomb was a hotshot financier who made millions before he was thirty-five. Used to date a nice girl, thought she might have been a nurse. The guy remembered her from a couple of parties. Then Whitcomb disappeared, and that was that. No one else knew anything."

"Billie, the bartender at the Club, said that Charlie seemed to want to keep you close at the party and wanted to know if you two were, well, you know. I told him I knew nothing about it, and what you did was nobody's business anyway."

Angie frowned and took a mouthful of coffee. "Jake, there is no such thing as privacy in this town!"

"Andy, a guy who knows Kevin, the fella who brought this Ben, said you two knew each other a while ago. Charlie looked a little pissed and left pretty quick. And that's it."

Angie looked down and clasped her hands tight. Then she sat up straight and faced Jake.

"OK Jake. Ben and I knew each other very well a while ago, before Dan. We haven't been in touch for over twenty-four years until I met him on Saturday. We had coffee. We're having breakfast later this morning. We weren't just friends. We were engaged and he left me." Her voice broke a little. "And I never knew why, but I never forgot him. Now he's back, and I might make a goddam fool of myself. And I don't care."

Angie got up to leave, with tears in her eyes.

Jake took her in his arms and held her like a troubled child needing comfort.

"Honey, go easy on yourself. Whatever you do, it's because you think it's right. It'll work out or not, but if you have feelings for this Ben fella after all these years, well, he must be a special guy."

She felt better. "Tell Eileen I'll see you both tonight. Usual time?" Jake nodded with an encouraging smile. With a quick hug, she went back home.

It was close to seven-fifteen when Angie gave a last inspection to her outfit. The unseasonably warm spell of the last few days had broken and the day was October-cool. On the way to the shower, she passed her work underwear drawer and went to the one with her dressy lingerie.

The blouse she picked was white silk. A thin lacy bra wouldn't work, but the satin one with French lace straps would. It had cost a fortune, and she hadn't worn it for a long time. Matching panties would be fine under her lined gray wool midi skirt. No need for a slip. She added a burgundy ultrasuede vest and her favorite shoes, gray suede with two-inch heels, a little thicker than spikes.

After showering, and taking time to be careful about her makeup, Angie gave herself a good spritz of Allure by Chanel before she dressed.

Her gold chain with a custom pendant and large gold knot earrings finished things off.

Beautiful underwear and good perfume always made Angie feel more confident. *And I damn well need to feel very confident, and just a little sexy, today.*

She had a presentation at the library as part of a panel discussion about "How to Get What You Need in the Age of 12 Minute Doctor Visits." Because there were four other speakers, Angie did a bulleted handout for her talk. The main points were:

- Write down in detail exactly what brought you to the office: pain, nausea, blood, being tired, trouble breathing, funny heart beats, a bad cold or whatever you have;
- Tell how long you've had the problem and if it's gotten better or worse;
- Bring a list of medications and your insurance card with a referral if it's required;
- Say if you've tried anything to make yourself better;
- Ask questions until you understand exactly what the doctor, Nurse, PA, or NP tells you;

- Be sure to get after-hours contact information in case you need help after the office is closed.

The mostly older adult audience was attentive, and gave the panel a good round of applause. Several people stayed to ask questions and two asked for her card.

It was nine-thirty when Angie finished. She had just the right amount of time to get to Vianni's after a quick check on her make-up.

CHAPTER 13

BREAKFAST

Ben took no chances that Angela would arrive at Vianni's first. He was in the parking lot forty minutes early, sitting in his Land Rover, reading the *Wall Street Journal*. At about twenty to ten, he went in to look for a spot with some privacy. *We're not going to need an audience watching while I tell her what she needs to know.*

The little restaurant reminded him of the picturesque cafes they used to enjoy for morning coffee. He liked it immediately and asked for a table outside on the patio. There was nobody else sitting there.

Clusters of large yellow and maroon Chrysanthemums sat in clay pots on a terrazzo floor. The round wooden tables set with heavy white cups and plates, thick silverware and dark green placemats made a pretty scene. Aromas of brewing coffee and freshly baked breads perfumed the air.

Vianni himself brought coffee and menus.

Angie came in ten minutes later. She was early too. Ben nearly knocked over his chair in his rush to stand. He relaxed a little when he saw her smile as she walked toward him.

How can he always look so elegantly handsome? That green plaid cotton shirt with the brown corduroys and boat shoes looks like an outfit out of Town and Country. Is that a Rolex?

It felt natural for him to skip the handshake and lean down to barely brush her cheek with a light kiss.

They had the same thought. *That was nice.*

When she gave him a little hug in return he was happily surprised. *Of course, it was a hug without much body contact, but it was spontaneous.*

He pulled out a chair for her, not quite all the way across the table, but not right next to him either. He hadn't said a word yet.

"So, are you going to say 'Good Morning,' Ben?"

"Of course. I was just a bit dazzled by how lovely you look even on a work day."

Dammit! He still looks straight into my soul with those eyes. That hint of a British accent only adds to his appeal. I need to remember why I'm here and not get distracted.

"Thank you. You look impressive yourself." Her smile was genuine.

As soon as they sat, Vianni returned with a white coffee pot, butter, jelly, croissants just out of the oven, and a small pot of hot water.

"Oh my, this is wonderful," she complimented the proprietor with a smile that brightened his day.

"The gentleman was quite specific about what I should bring." He gave a little formal bow and left them alone.

"He always reminds me of the café owners in Italy," she remarked, "a bit chubby, but immaculate in their white starched aprons over white smocks. He's part of the charm this place has."

Between sips of coffee and bites of croissant, they chatted about the party, where they had met for the second time in as many days. Ben told her how good it felt to see Jim and Nan again, while Angie commented that he seemed right at home.

Vianni returned, asking if they would like to order.

"I'm starved. Just realized I haven't eaten since last night. I get grumpy when I'm not fed!"

"Well, we wouldn't want that, Angela. You being grumpy can be terrifying!" *Oh hell! That slipped out. I should never have referred to what I remembered from the past. Will it make her upset before I explain anything?*

"You said the omelets were great. Would you like one?" He just stopped himself from asking if she still liked tomato and Swiss cheese.

He remembers everything! I can't deal with that conversation yet. I need a few minutes.

"Yes." She turned to Vianni. "A two-egg tomato and cheese omelet, a little more well done than usual, please."

Ben noticed how pleasant she was to the old man, and how he beamed at her in return. *She's a charming lady. Interesting she didn't let me order for her. Well, this isn't a date, I guess. But I think she's become a very independent woman.*

He ordered a three-egg omelet with bacon and Avocado. They drank more coffee before he put his mug down, turned his body toward her, and looked directly into her eyes. He put his hand on her forearm very lightly to emphasize the importance of what he was going to say.

"It really has been a long time, hasn't it Angela?" She opened her mouth to comment, but he stopped her with a soft, "Shhh. I need to tell you some things."

She sat very straight, unconsciously tensing every muscle in her body. Her first instinct was to get up and run out of there. She was terrified of what he might say. *What if he's with someone else? Why am I even giving that a thought? I don't give a damn. How could I after so long? Oh my god. I feel like I'm going to pass out.*

She shifted her body to face him, and started to speak again, but stopped at the look on his face.

"Angela, listen to me, please." He kept his hand on her arm.

"Ben it was all a lifetime ago. We survived and went on. Is it even a good idea to revisit such a horrible time?" *I can't take this. I thought I needed to know, but I'm not sure I can bear to think about the hurt.*

He interrupted her frantic thoughts when he took his hand away. Stone-faced, he asked, "Don't you care about what happened at all back then?" His voice was low, sad and disappointed.

Angie was silent for a minute before she responded with pain and anger in her voice. "Yes. I still care. All those years ago, I would have died to know. I loved you and you abandoned me with no explanation. It was as if you stabbed me through the heart and left me wounded, bleeding and in unbearable pain. I spent a long time trying to figure out what went on."

He took the brunt of her low-voiced barrage without flinching.

"Eventually, I buried the hurt and tried to hate you, but that didn't work. In the end, I was able to stop thinking about us for the most part and managed to have a good life."

She continued to look at him steadily, not allowing herself to show any mercy at the misery reflected on his face.

"So yes, Ben, I still care very much, but not enough to relive the excruciating memories." She was horrified to feel her eyes moisten. "I think I should leave before I make more of a fool of myself than I have." She reached for her purse.

All he wanted to do was comfort her in his arms and tell her he was sorry, but he knew she wouldn't allow that. Instead, he appealed to her logic.

"Didn't you invite me for breakfast mostly to get some answers? This is your chance. Please, Angela, stay long enough to hear what happened. You'll be able to put any uncertainty to rest at least. Don't you want that? And, for the record, you have not made a fool of yourself. You've been remarkably civil considering that I was so stupid and cruel."

She didn't trust herself to speak, but sat back, seeming to reconsider leaving.

He had the good sense to stay quiet while she decided what to do.

CHAPTER 14

ANSWERS

They sat in silence, looking at each other, for a minute or two.

Finally, Angie spoke, her voice barely audible. "OK Ben. I did ask you here to get some answers. Mostly." She paused and looked away. She didn't say more, but admitted to herself, *what I didn't realize was how much I'd enjoy just being with you again.* "You're right. We're here and this is the time. What happened?"

Vianni was on his way out with the omelets, but looked at the couple and turned to put them in the warmer for another few minutes. He'd make more if whatever was going on between them took that long. "They may not want them at all," he muttered to nobody in particular.

Ben drew in an audible breath. He sipped water and began his story.

"Angela, when I arrived in London, my sister, Emily, met me at the airport. Her husband was about to be sent to jail for securities fraud. She was distraught. Our stepfather told her she could come home, but on the condition that she get a divorce immediately. She and Marc had no money left after all of the lawyers' fees. To make things more complicated, she still loved the bastard!"

"I tried to convince Father to help them pay for an appeal, but he was having no part of it. Apparently, this wasn't the first time Marc needed bailing out. Mum didn't want to overturn her whole life by fighting with Father, so she was no help."

"Ben..." Angie started to respond.

"No, Angela, don't say anything yet. Let me tell you this. Please." He was paler, and his eyes were red.

"Monday morning I gave them the money to hire a barrister. The new team arranged to keep Marc out of prison pending the appeal. On the way home from a meeting with their lawyers, he ran a light and they were both killed by an oncoming bus."

Angie's eyes widened. She gasped and put her hand over Ben's fist, which was clenched on top of the table.

"I arrived on Sunday evening. My only sister and her rotter of a husband were dead by Tuesday night. They left twin boys a year old. Long story short, my stepfather wouldn't hear of adopting them."

"That's awful, Ben." She leaned toward him instinctively to touch his shoulder.

"Marc had no relatives. I made a decision on the spot that I would look after them until other arrangements could be made. I did it without asking you because I couldn't see a choice. Everything was a mess. I felt I couldn't ask you to give up your career and move to a new country with a ready-made family in a state of disaster."

Ben's face was ashen now. His hands were still white-knuckled on the table but he was looking directly at Angie to see her response.

She was quiet for a full minute with tears filling her eyes.

"Ben, I have to ask something."

He nodded and bowed his head.

"Why didn't you at least tell me what was going on then, instead of shutting me out? That was unspeakably cruel."

He looked up and saw the pain in her expression.

"Because I didn't have anything of myself to give to you, Angela. I had to hold everything in, wrap myself in armor and concentrate every ounce of sanity I still had on managing the whole horror story. My mother had sort of a breakdown and had stopped speaking, Father shut down. The boys had only their young nanny, and she was devastated too."

She nodded. *I kind of get that response after an overwhelming tragedy. It was what I did to cope too. Work, Gym, and Bingo the rescue cat. I couldn't handle anything else.*

"I was as beastly cruel as I could be to make you hate me and never try to track me down. If you managed to, you'd have been saddled with a man half-mad, trying to cope with two babies, a bereft nanny, and a family disaster. I was afraid that you'd feel stuck, and totally miserable, and I couldn't bear the thought."

"You should have given me a chance to support you, Ben."

"I know that now. Back then, though, my thinking was more insane than rational. I eventually realized my terrible mistake, and decided to see if you'd even consider talking to me. But it was too late. You were just married. I had hurt you terribly once, and it was out of the question for me to interfere with the life you had made for yourself."

And what would I have done? Left Dan and run off to London? Or stayed out of a sense of duty and faked our marriage while thinking about you? Maybe you did the right thing then.

He let his hand rest lightly on one of hers.

"And now, here we are. I know I can't expect forgiveness, ever. But do you at least understand a little?"

Damn right, you can't expect me to wipe all of that hurt away after a fifteen-minute conversation. But I am sad for what happened to you, and to us. It's still like an open wound.

Angie didn't even try to stop the tears running down her face. Ben wiped them with his napkin.

She took his hand in hers. "Oh Ben, I'm so glad you told me. The twins are the sons you mentioned when we had coffee?"

"Yes, and I never regretted adopting them. We rather learned about growing up together. I eventually married their nanny, more out of convenience than anything else. We never considered having children together. She was a lot younger than I was, and eventually found someone she truly loved. We divorced very amicably several years ago. We're all still very close. The boys consider her little girl their sister, and her husband as their uncle."

"What I do regret, quite bitterly, is not including you in things. It was selfish, stupid, and disrespectful. No matter what happened between us, it would have been better than hurting you the way I did."

By now, Ben had pulled his chair closer to her and his eyes pleaded with her to believe him.

"I never forgot you, Angela. You were the love of my life."

I'm so goddam mad, I could spit right now, even though I do understand a little. He as good as murdered me. So why do I want to hold him? Why am I as glad as I am mad? Because I'm still re-membering what we had together years ago. And he's still gorgeous, and gentle, and now, so sad.

Go slow, girl. Maybe he still bolts when things get tough.

"And now, Ben, is there a woman in your life?"

I have balls to ask that. But I have a right to know. I'm finished if making amends is all he wants. But I don't want to run away from him anymore. Oh, geez, this could be big trouble.

"There have been several women over the years, and there is someone now. It was a friend with benefits thing. The benefits stopped a while ago. I didn't want her to get the idea that we were heading toward a future together."

"OK Ben. We're normal adults. Of course we have lives, and friends, with and without benefits."

Why the hell did I say that? Because I want him to think there's someone else who wants me, that's why!

He looked at her lovely face, attractive body, and lis-tened to her voice. It was deep for a woman, and the way she spoke was compelling.

"Angela, just let me ask this. Would you consider see-ing me again, on whatever terms you choose? I know I have no right to ask. You have every reason to want me out of your life forever. Here's the thing though. I've never been able to fully commit to another woman since we were together. Maybe we're not compatible at all now. On the other hand, maybe there's a chance for us. Isn't it worth finding out?"

They were both thinking the same thing. *Yes, oh yes. Damn the consequences.*

"Well, we do seem to enjoy each other's company, don't we?"

Ben's face lost the pallor, and the smile that started in his eyes spread all over his face. "Yes, Angela, we do."

Her tears were gone, replaced by a smile and a light blush.

"There will be ground rules though, Ben. We'll take things very slowly, and accept that we both have lives, commitments, and other friends."

He nodded an enthusiastic yes. "Do you want that in writing, Angela?"

She gave him a playful tap on the hand. "No Sir, I trust your word is good."

Vianni had been watching the tableau. Smiling to himself, he appeared with fresh omelets and apologized for the wait.

Angie realized he probably observed the whole scene, and looked down in embarrassment. She never considered that anyone else had seen her and Ben.

Liliana and her client slipped out the front door unnoticed.

CHAPTER 15

CONNECTING

Angie had roller coaster feelings after Ben told her what had really happened all those years ago. She was ecstatic that he had never forgotten her, and yet furious at the way he dealt with the situation.

Consciously or not, he had chosen to carve her heart to pieces rather than explain things. That was something she didn't know how she'd resolve.

Maybe the past will take care of itself. I want to enjoy the moment for now. Here we are, having breakfast the way we used to do. OK, maybe we're not basking in an afterglow, but I still can't stop smiling.

"You must be thinking happy thoughts." He broke into her daydream.

Her response was out before she could stop herself. "This is fun. We must've changed over the years, but right now, we're connecting. I'm looking forward to getting to know you again." Her eyes sparkled.

Ben reached over and took her hand. He didn't attempt to cover his delight. "I wish we had champagne, Angela. This calls for a celebration."

"Another time, Ben. Right now, I need to go. I have mounds of paperwork to do."

"Fine. I want to know exactly what you do, when you have time to tell me. Whatever it is seems to keep you very busy, but happy. Will you be able to make time to see me again soon?"

"I think that can happen." Angela wanted to know some things too. "Are you staying nearby?"

"I'm condo sitting almost across the street from here, that new one on the shore. We're probably not far away from each other." *Actually about three miles from the address I sneaked a look at the other day. I wonder if you'd be upset that I did that?*

"Oh, the 'Plover Dunes'? That's a gorgeous place. I have a friend who moved there."

"Yes, well, if you need to go, let me walk you to the car and let's decide when we can start this slow process of catching up with each other." Ben was in no hurry, yet, to talk about the friend who owned that condo. He held her chair as she stood.

Vianni hurried to the door to say "Grazie." The bill was forty dollars. Ben left a twenty-dollar tip. "It pays to make customers happy," Vianni remarked aloud.

Ben guided Angie to the parking lot, with his hand lightly on the small of her back. It was the gesture of a solicitous gentleman.

Oh, that feels good. I'm out of my mind to let myself react this way. What's the harm though? It's just about high noon in a very public place. It can't go any further.

Ben felt her shiver a little and hid his smile. *Good! She does have a feeling or two lurking around.*

She slipped from his touch when they reached her BMW. "This is mine."

"Sharp wheels. It suits you...sporty, yet full of class. Are you free, let's see, any night from tomorrow on?"

Angie laughed. "Ben, what don't you get about slow? How about Friday or Sunday?"

He noticed that Saturday wasn't an option. *Wonder if Charlie has anything to do with that?*

"Would you be OK with something casual on Friday evening and then something special on Sunday? Maybe go somewhere for the day? Will you give me your cell number so we can firm things up during the week?"

"Wait a sec, Friday and Sunday too? Are we pushing things a little?" She couldn't help a teasing smile.

"Well," he said with a raised eyebrow and a wicked grin, "Friday can be a trial run. If we have a terrible time together, we'll reconsider Sunday."

She laughed at his clever excuse for making two dates.

"OK. We can do Sunday too, as long as Friday night isn't a disaster," she told him. "Here's my card. May I borrow a pen to write my home and cell numbers?"

He handed her a sleek green Mont Blanc ballpoint. When she finished writing, he took the card and put it in his wallet.

"Oh, by the way, where do you live, Angela?"

"Over in Rock Harbor on Terrace Road, 175. We're close to each other. How long will you be condo sitting here?"

"Only another few weeks. My flat in the Cambridge house is nearly ready. I'll miss Plover Cove though...nice people, good sailing, old friends nearby..." He let his voice trail off.

"Yes, well, ciao, old friend. I really do need to get back to work."

Neither of them could decide who leaned in first. They kissed, gently, and blissfully, with closed lips lingering. Ben held Angela's shoulders for just a moment when they finished. Her eyes were shining. So were his.

Liliana had stayed in her Mercedes. She usually made notes on her laptop after every client meeting.

That's the only reason I'm still in the lot. I'm not spying. They're certainly not trying to hide anything. No reason not to mention their little breakfast to an interested party if the time seems right.

Back at the office, Angie's office manager greeted her admiringly. "Hey, you look like the morning went super-well. Love that outfit! I haven't seen anything so chic around here for a good while."

"Thanks, Helen. I thought I could use some sprucing up. Fall always inspires me. Any messages?"

The other woman went to her desk and looked at a pad of paper.

"You had a couple of calls. I left notes on your desk. One was from Charlie, said he'd like you to call his cell ASAP. He'll be available to answer all afternoon. Otherwise, nothing else urgent."

Angie went into her office, closed the door, and kicked off her shoes. She hung her vest on a hanger. This was going to be a paperwork afternoon and she wanted to be comfortable.

Charlie. Now this is going to be tricky. We planned to have dinner at the club Saturday with Nan and Jim. I'm going to have to tell him that Ben is in the picture. It wouldn't be fair not to.

He answered on the first ring.

"Hi there, what's going on?" He usually texted, and she wondered what the occasion for a call might be.

"Hi, yourself, Gorgeous. Nothing special. Just thinking about you. Got time for a quick drink after work?"

"Oh, can't tonight, Charlie. I'm having dinner with Jake and Eileen. Sorry."

"OK then, maybe tomorrow? How about an early dinner at the Rock Harbor Pub? Nothing fancy, just burgers and wine?"

"Yes, sure. Meet you there around six. Sounds like fun. Are you sure nothing's on your mind?"

"Yep. At least nothing that can't keep 'til then. Take care, Angela."

Angie was floored. In all the time she'd known Charlie, he'd never called her anything but 'Angie' or 'Ange'. *Where did the 'Angela' come from? Oh my god. He heard Ben call me that. He smells something. I've got to get ahead of this. Charlie has women friends. He shouldn't be bent out of shape because I have a male friend. Right.*

Enough with the goddam drama. I have work to do.

She spent the rest of the afternoon writing proposals for client care, answering emails, and working on a new brochure.

By five, she was more than ready to spend some time with Jake and Eileen. *Jake will be panting to hear about breakfast today. Wonder what he told Eileen?*

⇥⊹⇤

After their breakfast, Ben watched Angie drive out of the lot. He sat in his Land Rover for a few minutes, thinking.

She felt something when I touched her back as we walked to the cars. I didn't imagine that little shiver. It's a good sign that she didn't pull away. Bet we still have some chemistry. I sure as hell felt something.

She's right though. We need to get to know each other again, I guess. Of course we've changed. We'll need to make some compromises. He shifted in his seat. *No, she has a career and a full life now. I'm the one who'll have to find a way to be part of things.*

Then, there're the boys. They'll be in the picture too. I can't push things too fast. But we shouldn't waste time, either. We're not kids anymore. And this holding back could get to be a bitch real soon. I feel as if this is a second chance for us.

"So don't screw this up, Mate. It's your last chance," he said aloud. "And stop talking to yourself. The conversation's not that brilliant."

CHAPTER 16
EILEEN AND JAKE

"Now, don't jump all over Angie asking her about this morning, Jake."

"Eileen, honey, give me some credit. I won't push. Don't think I've seen Angie cry since Dan's funeral, until today. Besides, we have some whopper of a news flash ourselves don't we?" Jake gleefully took her in his arms and danced around the oval-shaped dining room.

Eileen Hughes giggled, to Jake's delight. Standing as straight as she could, her head came only to his muscled shoulder. She had to tip it almost all the way back to look at him.

In all the years they'd been a couple, Eileen never tired of seeing his handsome face with high cheekbones, or running her fingers through his head of longish, bushy, snow white hair. She loved the way he laughed and how his blue eyes still smoldered when they made love.

They met at a wedding fifteen years before. Jake was sixty-five then. He had been a widower for four years and she was divorced for two. In her early fifties, Eileen was none too optimistic about her future.

Her son was twenty-five, independent and living in Hawaii. They saw each other only once a year. Jake had a son too, and they were very close until he was killed in a light plane crash five years before he met Eileen. Jake was convinced his wife died of a broken heart.

It took only a few dates for them to realize they never seemed to run out of things to talk about. In a year, they were together on weekends. Now, he spent at least one or two more nights at Eileen's and she spent one night at Jake's.

Rock Harbor was a small town and everyone knew what was going on. Both men and women cheered for the couple. Eileen retired from her nursing career a few years ago but drove people to doctor's appointments and took care of pets when owners were having health problems. Jake was involved in politics and did little home repairs if someone was in a fix. They considered their kindnesses a part of being good neighbors.

People figured there was some reason they never married, but nobody thought it was because they didn't adore each other.

The table sparkled with antique china and sterling. *Why keep beautiful things for best, at our age. Besides, this is a real celebration night and we should be festive.* She was as excited as Jake to tell Angie their plans.

Her peacock blue silk shirt with a matching long print skirt complemented short, soft, curly gray hair. Diamond stud earrings, a present from Jake, were her only jewelry. They were a contrast to nearly black eyes that always seemed warm.

"Hey Jake, have you changed yet? Put on the yellow shirt. You always look great in that."

He chuckled. After his wife died, Jake's standards for clothes were, did it fit? Was it clean?

Eileen had a different take on his appearance. She expressed her feelings about six months into their relationship. "You're too damn handsome not to pay a bit more attention to how you look, Mister," she told him.

Slowly, Jake's wardrobe expanded with comfortable, classic clothes in his favorite colors. He agreed to a new navy blue blazer to replace his old brown check. When he needed a suit for a wedding, Eileen found a skilled tailor who had excellent fabrics, a casually friendly attitude, and reasonable prices.

He heard, "Hey, Jake, looking good there, man," more than once when he was out. He rather liked it.

Jake slid the yellow shirt and brown wool trousers off their hangers, dressed quickly, added a dash of light aftershave, and headed to help Eileen in the kitchen.

Wrapped in a massive apron, she was whisking some salad dressing. Jake opened a can of anchovies for the Caesar Salad.

"Can't decide which smells better, Love…the bread or your special chicken in wine." Jake kissed the top of Eileen's head.

"Well, Angie loves that chicken. We don't know what kind of day she's had. Let's pamper her a bit."

The doorbell rang and Jake was quick to answer it.

"Angie, honey, you look gorgeous. And you didn't have to bring wine." He gave her a gentle bear hug.

She wore the silk blouse and midi and added a patent leather belt studded with bits of silver. Eileen always looked lovely, so Angie decided against changing into jeans.

"You're quite the handsome dude yourself, Jake. Color's perfect for you. I brought red and white. Wasn't sure what we were having."

"Your favorite chicken, Angie." Eileen appeared, apron gone, with a warm smile. She kissed Angie on the cheek.

"OK then ladies, let's start with a drink to shed the day's worries."

Relaxed in the living room, with comfortable furniture in shades of cream and green, the three were ready to talk.

Jake wasn't going to wait. "Eileen, we going to tell Angie, or what?"

"Heavens, Jake, can't you wait 'til dinner?"

"Nope. Tell her!"

"Enough, you two. Tell me now. You're both so happy, I think I should have brought champagne."

"Angie, dear, Jake and I have decided that we've lived apart long enough. We're moving in together full time. We'll live here in Jake's house, because it's bigger and closer to the center of town."

"That's wonderful! I'll have the two of you for neighbors. Oh, congratulations!" She got up and kissed them with genuine joy.

"Honey, that's not all. We're not getting married, but we're having a Commitment Service at Old South. We want you to be our witness. Would you do that?"

"Oh Jake, Eileen, I'd be so honored. Thank you for asking." She had tears in her eyes, and they did too.

"No crying. Let's have dinner, then a sinful dessert. We have the champagne." Eileen led them into the dining room.

During the meal, they told Angie the ceremony would be in about a month, and after the church, there would be a small but elegant celebration at the club. It closed the first of November and theirs would be the last function of the season.

"I'm not selling the house immediately," Eileen told her. "I plan to rent it for a while. Prices are going up and I've been advised to wait a little. Liliana says she can get about twenty-five hundred a month easily. That should cover my board and room." She flashed a smile at Jake, who looked appalled.

"None of that rent-paying nonsense, Love. You'll buy yourself something nice with that money!" Angie laughed out loud.

"Eileen, can I show her?"

"You will anyway Jake, so go ahead."

He pulled a small box from his pocket and opened it. Angie gasped. Two rows of diamonds encircled the entire ring in about three carats of brilliance. She had seldom seen anything that beautiful. "Oh, Eileen, Jake, it's magnificent. May it always reflect your happiness."

After a glass of champagne, Jake cleared his throat. "Angie, honey, you've heard our news. You have anything we might be interested in hearing?"

"Jake! If Angie wants to say something, she will. And we'll listen. Quietly."

"Well, yes. I might have a quick bulletin for you. I assume Jake has filled you in on what I did for breakfast today, Eileen?"

"He did mention something, Dear. You were a bit anxious about things, as I understood it."

Angie couldn't keep a straight face. "Oh, Eileen, you're such a diplomat. I'm delighted with how things went. It felt right being with Ben. Breakfast was wonderful. And it's not the bubbly talking."

The older couple looked happy and relieved.

"Ben told me what happened all those years ago. He walked into a family tragedy, starting at the airport when he arrived. He made some split second decisions as things got worse, and some of them, the ones about us, were wrong. In his words, he was 'half-mad,' for a long time. When he finally got to where he could try to fix things, it was way too late. He found out that I was just married, and he didn't want to upend my world for a second time."

Very softly, Eileen asked, "And can you forgive him for those bad decisions?"

"I'm not sure about forgiving him, but it was a long time ago, and so much has happened to both of us. If it comes to that, I hope I can live with what happened. Honestly, from what I've seen, I want to get to know Ben more. He told me he was delighted with that, and agreed to take things very slowly. He knows we're probably very different from what we were. I'm going to be careful. I will not allow him or anyone else to hurt me like that again. Ever." Her lips were set in a firm line.

Jake kept his thoughts to himself. *She's already half loopy about this guy. He'd better treat her right, or he'll be dealing with me.*

Eileen didn't dare catch his eye. She could guess what he was thinking.

When they finished dinner, all three brought plates into the kitchen. Jake suggested that Angie and Eileen have a glass of champagne in the sunroom while he took care of the dishes.

"Eileen cooked, I clean up," he said. "I'll join you in a bit." He got a kiss from each of the women and shooed them off.

They sat in the same spot where Jake had comforted Angie that morning.

"I'm going to give you some unsolicited advice now, Dear. You're like my little sister, so please don't be angry at this."

"Eileen, I know seeing Ben again after what he did might be foolish and maybe dangerous, but…"

"Hush Dear. Jake and I spent much too much time being careful. I loved him less than two weeks into our relationship, and I'm sure he felt the same way. We didn't sleep together for nearly a year. I still regret that time we wasted."

"You said that you were going to be careful. Don't be so careful he feels you're not interested. I can tell you are. I know there were some tough times in your marriage, even though you and Dan had a good life. He had his moods."

"Taking a chance to find out what you and Ben might have sounds like it's worth the consequences. I'm finished, now, Dear."

Angela took Eileen's hand and kissed it. "Thank you, big Sis."

Of course, Jake had been eavesdropping, and he agreed with everything Eileen said. After a decent interval, he appeared with a second bottle of champagne and some chocolate truffles.

Angie knew she'd be late for work on Wednesday, but she wasn't seeing clients until the afternoon.

CHAPTER 17
CAMBRIDGE HAPPENINGS

After breakfast with Angela, Ben was spending the rest of the day in Cambridge to check on the house and have dinner with his sons. He'd ignored the dozen or so apologies Ollie texted over the last two days. *Maybe by now, she's finally got the message not to involve the boys in whatever games she's playing.*

He had to admit, it was fun to see her every now and again, and she didn't attempt to rekindle the physical relationship until this last time. She even seemed to back off when he said he wasn't interested in one-night stands.

Since I agreed to stay at her condo until she's back in town, I can't cut her off completely anyway. Besides, I doubt Angela will drop Charlie. She was right when she said we're adults, and we are entitled to have friends. He decided to text Ollie before starting the drive to Cambridge.

Hi, Not still mad at u. Need to talk tho. Late lunch n NY Sat? Got to b back here Sat. nite. Plaza OK? Ben

He was sure she'd answer soon enough.

Traffic from Plover Cove to Cambridge was usually heavy, but he thought he had plenty of time before seeing the designer and contractor, a father and daughter team. They were scheduled to meet at three. It sounded as if his flat would be ready in the next couple of weeks. There was no big rush because he was obligated by his commitment to Ollie until around the first of November.

The house was a legal three-family, off Central Square, in a Cambridge neighborhood that used to be considered poor. It had three spacious apartments when Ben bought it. The permits for extensive renovations and condo conversion were in place. He decided to let Ryan and Pete each have a flat. The third one would be a convenient spot for him when he was in the Boston area. It was a layout that would work well if he wanted to sell separate units in the future.

He hadn't specifically mentioned to Angela that he had a large home in Naples Florida and an office there, as well as a small town house and office in London. The business card he had given her listed both, but she didn't ask anything. *Considering the importance of all that we discussed this morning, I never gave it a thought.*

Ben found drivers in Cambridge were more aggressive than almost anywhere in the world, maybe with the exception of Rome or Paris. He tapped the horn as a bike swerved directly into the Land Rover's path. The cyclist flashed a middle finger as he snaked away through the snarled traffic.

Damn it! Now I know why people say to drive around here before six in the morning or after eight at night. This trip from Plover Cove, even taking all the short cuts and back streets, is mad. But, it'll be good seeing the boys. Nice that they still like to touch base in person, even if it is a rare event.

He arrived at the house two and a half hours later. The drive would have taken less than an hour without the awful traffic. He survived several near misses with pedestrians listening to something through ear pods, and avoided more cyclists slithering through red lights and traffic jams.

"Hey, Ben, howzit goin'?" Mike Collins, his contractor was waiting on the front porch.

He parked in the wide driveway and got out, shaking his head. "OK except for the horrific traffic you folks around here have."

"Aw, ya get used to it." Mike slapped Ben on the back and then looked apologetic.

"Nellie's stuck on the bridge in some kinda traffic mess. She'll be along in about twenty minutes. We can look at the construction stuff first, then you'll be ready to talk to her about the space and décor."

"I don't wonder she's stuck, Mike. Everything's gridlocked from Revere on in. No worries, I'm meeting Ryan and Pete at six. Maybe we can get a drink before then after the business talk is done."

Mike and his daughter, Nellie, were a great team. She started to go with her Dad to building sites when she was four, and loved every minute of it. A flair for decorating and designing came out as early as middle school. Now, at 24, she could spot a construction problem immediately. That came in very handy when she was planning and working on a project.

The walk-through went without any problems. Ben reviewed all of the permits and inspection results. Everything was perfect. Even though Nellie was in charge of showing him the décor and layout, he noticed the flow and finishes as he talked to her dad.

A Volvo wagon pulled in behind Ben in the driveway. Nellie hopped out, a long blonde ponytail swinging with her motion as she loped up the stairs. Comfortable jeans and a pink polo allowed easy movement, but did not disguise her tall, graceful body.

"Crap! Pop, Ben, sorry to be late. Some dumbass cut in as he was coming onto the bridge too fast from a ramp. Rear-ended a guy and of course, I was just behind the mess. Got held up for half-an-hour."

"No problem, Hon, Just got this guy's approval on all but your end of things, so let's get moving."

They walked into the first floor unit.

"Ben, have you talked to Ryan and Pete at all over the last week or so?" Nellie was casual in the way she asked the question.

"Not much, something up?"

"Just wondered if all of you are on the same page, colors, fixtures. You know."

"Nellie, they'll use the bedrooms and the baths, maybe a coffee maker every day. Pete likes to cook if he has friends in, but Ryan eats from a stack of take-out menus."

"Yeah. Pete cooks better than I do."

Mike and Ben looked surprised at her comment.

Soft neutral colors played well with a huge bow window in the large multi- purpose front room. Sun flooded in, making the hard wood floors shine. A smaller, informal room sat on the opposite side of a large foyer. It accommodated enough furniture for a study group to meet comfortably. A computer, printer and other electronics sat on a big desk.

While walls were open, Ben had the house wired to accommodate smart house technology.

The well-equipped kitchen flowed from the smaller room and had a second entrance coming from a short hall. Nellie had done it in whites and creams with brushed nickel pulls echoed in pendant lights over a peninsula. A powder room was off the foyer, and each of the two large bedrooms had adjoining baths.

The décor was calm, warm, and punctuated with splashes of color in area rugs and pillows.

All the units were alike, and Ben was delighted.

"Nellie, you've done a great job. I see Pete and Ryan have moved in."

She smiled at his sincere praise. "Yes, and the cleaning crew will have everything perfect by Monday. So, are you going to see Pete soon?"

"Yes. He and Ryan are having dinner with me this evening. Hey, why don't you and your dad join us?"

"Sorry, I can't." The beautiful young woman didn't meet his eyes, and gave no explanation.

Ben hoped there hadn't been any problems between Nellie and the boys.

"OK, but Mike and I are going for a drink now, how about..."

She interrupted. "I've got some stuff I need to do. Maybe another time?"

Nellie kissed her dad on the cheek, gave Ben a light hug and left rather quickly.

"Mike, any problems between Nellie and Ryan or Pete? She seemed kind of off about something."

"Nothing I know about. She's got a million irons in the fire. Probably just nervous about you seeing the finished product for the first time."

The two men decided that *The Scholar*, a local pub in the square, had the best beer selection in town. Ben put Nellie's behavior in the back of his mind.

CHAPTER 18

BOYS' SURPRISE

B en spent a pleasant hour tasting local craft beer and talking about Cambridge real estate with Mike. He headed back to the house for a final look, then drove to the Fire Phoenix for dinner with his sons.

"Hey, Dunk," he heard Pete, then saw him wave from a corner table in back. It was tucked away from the cheerful chaos in the open area of the restaurant.

"Guys! Great to see you." Ben's boys got up to hug him heartily.

"Yeah, Dunk, it's been a while." They sat, situating his chair so he could talk comfortably to both of them. Aromas from Peking Ravioli, Spring Rolls, Spare Ribs, Fried Shrimp, Crab Rangoon, and a huge tureen of soup wafted from the table.

"So how many are we feeding here, guys?"

"Dunk, we're still building muscle," Pete told him.

"Right," Ryan added. "And you like all of this. If we want more, we can always order full meals."

Ben just laughed.

"Besides, finger food is easier when you want to talk." Pete shot Ryan a look, unmistakably warning him to slow down.

Ben caught the vibe quickly. He knew something was going on but decided to let the young men take the lead.

The waiter arrived with a round of beers. "These're on Joe," he told them. "For good customers."

The tall, pleasant looking, young Asian man at the front entrance returned Ryan and Pete's wave of thanks.

"Joe's one of the owners Dunk. He takes good care of us."

"The lady not with you tonight?" the waiter asked.

"Nah, tonight's for the guys. We need to catch up," Ryan told him.

Ben caught the flush on Pete's face. *Wonder if he's the one with the lady? Usually it's Ryan. Well, he'll tell me when he's ready.*

Helping himself to a healthy plate of the appetizers, he asked his sons "Everything OK with the house? I was with Mike and Nellie this afternoon to see it. Flats look good. He took a bite of the well-flavored Crab Rangoon. "Nellie seemed to think I needed to catch up with you both on how things were going."

"It's great! Couldn't be better." Ryan answered. Pete quietly sipped his beer, but his face colored again.

What's going on with them and Nellie? Sure as hell, that reaction wasn't for Mike.

"So, Dunk. Not to be nosey, but you want to tell us what's up with Ollie? She's called a couple of times to say Hi. Said you two haven't been in touch a lot." Ryan was still doing most of the talking, but Pete was listening now.

"Hey, do I ask questions about your ladies? Like the one who's not with you tonight?"

"C'mon," it was Pete now. "Ollie's been around for a while. Kind of thought you two might have something going."

Ben took a minute to sip his beer and munch on more food. "Well, guys, we're good friends now. Maybe it was more once, but things don't always work in the long run." He carefully put down his chopsticks. "You can both rest easy about my social life though." His smile let them know he didn't mind the questions. "I met an old friend. Haven't seen her for a very long time. Need to sort some things out. I'll keep you posted."

The boys knew from his tone and careful expression, the conversation was over. As twins often do, they had the same thought.

We're going to want to know more about this old friend. But later'll be fine.

For the next few minutes, the three concentrated on enjoying the food. They took a break before deciding about more dishes.

"So, anything new with you two?" Ben asked.

The waiter appeared to clear the table and bring fresh beer. The young men looked at each other. Pete finally spoke with barely controlled glee.

"Well, Dunk, remember when you gave us the money for a project we were fooling around with in the rented garage a couple of years ago?"

"Yes. You guys were developing an app or something with robots, weren't you?"

Ryan chimed in. "Yeah. When we came up here, Pete brought in a few other guys for the technical development side, and it's gone really well. I've been doing some business plans. Wonder if you'd take a look?"

"Sure. Let me know when and where. You've got someone interested in your product?"

They weren't hiding their excitement very well.

"Well, we've had a couple of meetings with ICOS."

Ben sat up straight in his chair and put his beer down.

"Did you say ICOS? Is it the ICOS that's developing robots for health care?"

"Yep." Huge grins spread over both their faces.

"Have they made an offer?"

"They've thrown out general numbers and talked about both of us heading up the development of our own project. We need you to make sure we're not getting screwed, Dunk."

Ben was proud and astounded at what his sons had accomplished.

"What kind of numbers are we talking?"

Ryan, as the deal making part of the duo leaned over the table. "Maybe an initial ten mil payment for them to get rights to develop this specific technology, along with a salary and a piece of the profits for us. Of course they'll guarantee us a minimum yearly amount no matter if there's a profit or not, and a five year contract."

Ben refilled his glass and had another dumpling.

"Not bad at all. Let me do a little research. How long is the offer open?"

"We'd like to get back to them in a couple of weeks and wrap things up by mid-November or sooner," Ryan answered.

"OK, then. What about finishing grad school?"

"We've already arranged a leave with the option to return. And there is one other thing." Ryan looked serious.

"Yeah," Pete echoed. "We'd like to buy the Cambridge house from you. At a fair price, of course."

"Any particular reason? Are you looking for an investment?"

"Dunk," this time Pete pulled his chair a little closer. "Nellie and I, we've gotten to know each other really well."

Ryan choked on his soup. "You might say that, yeah."

Pete waved his brother off and continued, "Well, Dunk, she's moving in next week. If it's OK with you, we'd like to use the first floor for a work studio for both of us. Ryan agreed to move to the third floor. He's hardly there anyhow."

Ben reacted, "Pete, This is a big surprise! When did you start seeing each other?"

Good god! No wonder Nellie was so skittish today. Wonder if Mike knows? She's a wonderful girl, but how long has this been going on?

"We've been dating since the day she walked on the job six months ago. I asked her for coffee that afternoon and we really clicked. I think we're in love, Dunk."

"Well, after today's commute from Plover Cove, I won't miss living here. Although I need to be out of Ollie's condo before she comes back. Shouldn't be a problem to find a temporary spot though."

"Really Dunk? She wouldn't let you bunk on a couch or something?" Ryan teased, then added, "You can use my guest room for a while if you need to."

Ben cuffed him affectionately on the arm. "OK gents, here's how it's going down."

"First, congratulations on the deal to both of you." Then, "Pete, Nellie's a find. You're damn lucky I think. She is too, but women like her are rare. I had one once and was too dumb to handle it. Don't screw up son, if you're sure she's the one."

"Wait on buying the house for a while, maybe a few months. You can rent it from me. Perhaps we can get ICOS to throw the rent and purchase price into your agreement. It's not so unusual for companies to offer extra perks when they're dead set on buying an invention. If everything goes as well as it should, you can buy the place later if you still want to."

All three of them let out enough of a whoop to make Pete and Ryan's friend, the Fire Phoenix owner, come over to ask what they were celebrating. The four shared some Peking duck and a bottle of Moet champagne, both as a gift from the management.

After the beer and champagne, Joe decided none of the three should drive. They loaded the boys' bikes into Ben's Land Rover, and one of the waiters drove it to the Cambridge house. Joe chauffeured them home in his own vintage Cadillac convertible.

Ben stayed overnight. He fell asleep thinking that living North of Boston near the ocean could be very nice.

CHAPTER 19
ANGIE TELLS CHARLIE

Driving to work, Angie thought about her date with Charlie that evening. *He seems to want to talk about something important. Wonder what? Well, I won't have a lot of time to think about it today.*

She had a family meeting scheduled to discuss the kind of help that would make it safe and comfortable for Mr. and Mrs. Filmore to remain at home instead of moving to Assisted Living.

Raised voices coming from the conference room alerted her to problems before she joined the group.

Their son was making it clear he was through listening to his father. "Pop, this is bullshit!" he shouted, standing and leaning across the table. "You can't maintain the house on your own. Mom's done most of it over the years, and now it's too much. You've gotta move on hiring people or go someplace where you'll have help."

Both Angie and his wife spoke at the same time.
"Bill…"

"Shut up Rose," he yelled at his wife. "He's just selfish and cheap. He doesn't want to spend the money except for this fancy nurse who'll take his side."

"Mr. Filmore, let's talk a bit about what your parents have done so far," Angie started.

"They should have done a hell of a lot more by now. Either he gets off his duff and moves or I get him declared incompetent!"

Both his sisters stood up. "Like hell you will. You might be able to bully your wife, but not us," the older one told him.

Before Bill could retort, his father slammed a fist on the table.

."Enough. All of you, get out. You've upset your mother. Go. Now. Girls, we'll talk later."

His son shoved open the conference room door and slammed it as he left. Angie's team looked annoyed and concerned.

"Ms. Martin-Wilson, there may be a small bit of truth in what my son said," the senior Mrs. Filmore started.

"Elinore. Stop!"

"No, Gus. You stop. In sixty-five years of marriage, I let you take the lead. Now, I'll have my say."

"Elinore, we're leaving." The old man got shakily to his feet, red-faced, perspiring, and leaning heavily on his cane.

"Gus, if you leave now, don't come home." The elegant looking woman took a sip of coffee and leaned back in her chair. "You are cheap and you are asking too much of me and the kids."

He moved toward the door.

"Bill had no right to talk to you like that. I will not support him." She spoke to his back and her voice resonated. "However, you will not live in the house unless you come here and listen to Angie's list of people who can help us. Remember, you deeded that house to me several years ago for tax purposes."

He stopped, but didn't turn.

"Goddammit Gus! Stop being an old fool" Mrs. Filmore's shout filled the room.

Angie was startled, but decided not to intervene yet.

"Elinore! I have never heard you curse." Mr. Filmore finally turned, shock on his face.

"That's because you never bothered to listen. I took care of a house, raised three kids, and catered to you. Trust me, I cursed. A lot. I mean this, Gus. I love you, but I will not let you work me to death."

The old man's knees started to shake. "Ms. Martin-Wilson, I feel a bit weak."

Ken, the attorney on the team, was at his side before he finished the sentence. As soon as Gus was in his chair, there was hot tea in front of him, along with some soft biscotti that was always in the office.

After a few sips of tea and bites of the pastry, his color was normal and he had stopped perspiring. His wife had not made a move to help him. She sat, looking at her husband with determination.

"Well, Gus?"

"Elinore, you made your point. In a most unladylike way, but you have my attention."

"Oh good," she responded softly, with a charming smile.

"But Bill will have nothing to do with the plans. He will be removed as a co-executor."

"I agree," his wife responded.

"You are always a surprise, my dear. Ms. Martin-Wilson, how soon can you arrange for some help? I, no, *"we,"* can afford it. And, of course, we want to keep your services so Elinore won't have to worry about arranging anything else we might need."

Angela and the group had all the information ready. The Filmores would be fine.

She was exhausted after the two hours. Not that warring families were so unusual, but the son, Bill, was almost vicious. Ken may need to be more involved in this case than anyone else on the team.

Angie looked forward to a burger and wine with Charlie tonight. Although that would be another difficult conversation.

I have to tell him that Ben's in the picture. At least enough so he knows there's not a clear path to us getting more serious. However, do I really want him to think there's no chance for us? How can I be certain? Well, this isn't the time to think about it.

The rest of the day went by quickly. She was on her way to the pub by five-thirty. *I'll be early, but I could use a glass of wine before he arrives. I want to be relaxed.*

⥌⥑

Charlie was way ahead of Angie. He had selected seats in a corner, with a courtyard view. He knew she liked seeing the autumn chrysanthemums. Subtle lights created a pretty outside scene. When she walked in, he left some friends at the bar, and proudly escorted her to the prime table. A pleasant server appeared with a bottle of chilled Pinot Grigio, a plate of olives, and warm Bruschetta.

"Hey, Charlie, didn't you say we were having a burger and a beer tonight? This looks like a lot more. What's the occasion?"

"We in a hurry, Angie? Or do you prefer Angela?"

"I could be in a damn big hurry if you don't cut the crap, Charlie. I've had a tough day. Don't need a night of aggravation." She softened the remark with an impish smile. "Angie'll be fine."

"Try the wine. Harry, the bartender, says it's one of their best. Hell, might make you less touchy, even." He spooned ice into her wide goblet and poured wine, just as she liked it.

I am on edge, more than I realized. And he is being thoughtful, that's for sure.

"So, Charlie, everything OK? You sounded anxious yesterday when you called."

"Not really anxious, Angie. Just wanted to find out how well you actually know Ben Whitcomb. Well enough for a leisurely breakfast, anyway. That I did hear."

Well, someone saw us at Vianni's. I'm letting that crack pass. Here goes. "I knew Ben over twenty-five years ago Charlie, before Dan." She took a healthy sip of wine and ate an olive. "I knew him well."

Charlie hadn't touched his wine nor taken his eyes from her face.

"We unexpectedly met again recently, then at the club again last Sunday. We had some things to catch up on. I invited him to breakfast Tuesday. I learned what I needed to know."

Charlie drank some of his wine, popped a piece of Bruschetta into his mouth, and leaned toward her.

"Angie, I think there might have been something big between you two. And that's fine. None of my business. But you know I care for you. A lot."

This time, he reached over and took her hand. She didn't pull away. "I don't want you to be hurt. I don't think I want to lose you, either." He took his hand away. "But, if I'm not welcome to stick around, just tell me."

"Charlie, you are welcome in my life." She reached out and gently rubbed his hand. It was cold, she noticed. *He's tense!*

"Look. I won't lie to you," she continued. "We were very special to each other. It was a jolt to see him again. We have memories. Maybe there are some feelings between us still." She dropped her eyes. "But I'm not sure about anything. I don't think I'm ready to make big changes. I love my life and my friends."

Angie was horrified to feel her eyes filling up. She could feel tears spilling over and used her napkin to dry her face.

"Oh, goddammit, Charlie, I'm so confused. I can't make promises or decisions. I care a lot for you too. Ben and I are going to get to know each other again, and I can't consider sleeping with you if we're not going to be dating exclusively. If that's not enough for now, then I can't ask you to stick around." She couldn't stop the tears and turned her face toward the courtyard.

His mouth softened and his eyes widened. He couldn't remember seeing her cry before and he was astonished.

Damn this bastard Ben for upsetting our lives. He took the hand that she wasn't using to wipe her eyes.

"Angie, it's OK. Drink your wine, please don't cry. I'm not going anywhere. I'll be your friend without asking for anything else." *No way can I tell her what I found out about where he's living or who he's been dating. Not when she's this upset.*

"Please, take it easy. You need food."

"I'm really not hungry," she said between sniffles.

"I know what will make you feel better." He got up to find the server, gave the order, and told her to bring it in about fifteen minutes.

Angie had managed to stop crying and was nibbling at the appetizers when he returned. She gave him a shaky smile. "You are terrific, Charlie."

"Good. Are we still on for dinner with Nan and Jim Saturday night?"

"Are you up for it, considering everything?"

"I told you. I'm sticking with you until you tell me not to."

Her tears were gone. As requested, the server arrived with an unusual order.

"I figured this is just the thing when real food won't do," Charlie told her.

She laughed out loud. He had gotten her a plate of anchovies, a Caesar salad, Tiramisu, and some gelato.

They laughed for the rest of the evening. He never again mentioned Liliana's detailed report of Angie's breakfast with Ben and the parking lot kiss.

Charlie planned to stay in the game. He was getting too old for being the bachelor man about town and was thinking more and more seriously about giving up the other ladies. He walked Angie, happy and filled with sweets, to her car.

"I can't tell you how much I appreciate you being so understanding about all of this," she told him. Several steamy hugs and kisses, which she initiated and he returned with enthusiasm, showed she was sincerely grateful.

He handed her into the car and kissed the tip of her nose lightly. "Night, Gorgeous. Don't worry so much. Text me when you get home." He watched her drive out of the lot and then went back to the bar.

It's still early. I think I'll stop for another one with the guys.

Charlie heard Liliana before he reached his friends. "Hi, handsome. Can a lady buy you a drink?"

How long has she been at the bar? And how does she always look ready?

Liliana wore a conservative black suit. It was her bright green silk blouse with the three top buttons opened that Charlie noticed. There was just a peek of black lace showing.

Shit! Well, I haven't pledged fidelity yet.

"Sure, Lily. You hungry? We could grab a table."

"Or, we could have some single malt and cheese in my office, Charlie. As you know, it's quite comfortable."

Charlie smelled her perfume and couldn't resist. "Much better choice. Let's go."

CHAPTER 20

BEN AND MIKE

B en opened his eyes slowly. He was thirsty and his head
ached. Nine AM showed on the alarm. The smell of
fresh coffee wafted from somewhere. He jumped from bed
to the floor of an unfamiliar room.

*Oh yeah. It's Wednesday morning. I stayed in Ryan's guestroom.
I should have texted Angela last night. Well, maybe it's good I didn't.
She kept reminding me how we needed to take things slow. Wonder if
she enjoyed that little kiss in the parking lot as much as I did?*

His headache and rocky stomach reminded him he
couldn't drink and eat like a kid anymore. "I feel like crap,"
he said aloud.

"You kinda look like crap too." Ryan was at the door
with a cup of coffee and a snarky grin. "You're out of practice doing celebrations."

Ben just looked at his new millionaire son and grimaced.

"Bathroom's through that door, Dunk. Clean skivvies
are on the towel rack. Mike's in the kitchen. Wants to talk.
Doesn't have a gun or anything as far as I can see. Guess
Nellie had a chat with him last night."

"Any aspirin handy, Ryan?" Ben mumbled as he headed for the shower, "Maybe some tomato juice?"

"They're on the kitchen table. Grey Goose too."

After a long shower, ending with an icy rinse, Ben felt the hangover fading. He dressed, shaved, and went to join Mike for some conversation.

"You don't look so good." The concerned looking man was at the kitchen island with a glass in his hand. "Bloody Mary might help. Guess you got the news?"

"Yes. It was a big surprise, but I'm delighted for the kids. Pete couldn't be luckier. Never came even close to moving in with anyone before."

He took two aspirin and slugged down a full glass of tomato juice in one swig, leaving the vodka untouched for the moment.

"Nellie either. She's nuts about him, Ben. As long as she's happy, I'm OK with it, I guess. From everything I've seen, he seems like a swell kid."

Ben settled himself across the counter from the man who had become a friend during the house construction.

"She's your only daughter. If I were you, I'd want a full background check. He's a solid kid, Mike. Wouldn't take this kind of step if he didn't think Nellie was the one for him."

"Better not. Irish dads can get pretty pissed if their little girls are hurt."

"And no blame for that. I react dreadfully if I think someone is causing either of my boys worry or trouble. It's what dads do." Smiling, he added, "I'd probably have a squad of bodyguards and detectives on the payroll if I had a daughter." He gestured at Mike's empty glass. "How about another bloody? Might just join you."

As he made their drinks, Ben told him, "Looks like I'm going to be homeless in a while too. You know about the house, their business, and all?"

"Yep. Nellie told me the whole thing. She's going to work with Pete on the project and keep her work with me as well. The kids respect each other. They've formed a good team. Nice that Nellie and Ryan get along too. She says he's got a helluva business head. Hey, about the house. If you need something quick, I've got nice apartments in a few places close by."

Ben popped some bread in the toaster and put butter and jelly on the table for both of them. He poured coffee in thick white china cups as well. "Did Nellie pick out the dishes and other kitchen things too? Doubt that either of the guys have that kind of taste."

"She did." Her father answered. "Wonder if she was thinking ahead to what she'd want to live with? She and Pete have probably been making plans for a while now."

Ben laughed. "Kids. They keep us parents on our toes even when they're adults. You said you lost your wife. How long has it been just you and Nellie?"

"About six years now. She was eighteen, and finished her first semester at Northeastern. Technically, she was an adult, but she was real close to her mother. It was a rough time. My sister, Mae, stepped in and got us both through it. Damn! I bet she knew about this whole thing. Wouldn't break her word to tell me if Nellie made her promise not to."

Hoisting his glass, Ben gave a toast. "To all of our kids. May they have health, happiness, and prosperity. To us.

Sanity, patience, and a sense of humor." They drank more coffee and munched on toast.

"Thanks for the apartment offer, Mike, but you know, I kind of like Plover Cove on the North Shore. I work from home most of the time. Boston's close for meetings, and the airport is a few miles away. I might stay up there for a while. With the house in Naples, it'll be a nice combination."

"Pretty spot. Enough to do up there?"

"Yeah. I've met some folks. Can get into town whenever I want. I have to find a real estate agent fast. I'm condo-sitting but need to be out when my friend gets home."

The two men finished their food and talk. They clapped each other on the shoulders, feeling at ease. "Do you think you and your sister could make time for dinner after I straighten out where I'm going to live?"

"Great idea, Ben. She'd love it." Mike stretched. "You know, I'm not used to drinking in the morning. Think I'll go home and sleep for an hour. My crew will be glad I'm out of their hair. You drive careful, now. It's a bit of a ride."

When Mike left, Ben texted Pete and Ryan congratulating them again and saying he'd look over the agreements and give them his thoughts by Friday. He told Pete to give Nellie a hug for him.

At least traffic's not as bad going north. Glad I poured a very short shot into my Bloody Mary. We needed to chill, not get trashed. I'll be spending the rest of the day on these papers.

Ollie had answered his text almost immediately yesterday.

Looking forward to lunch Saturday. Will make three pm reservation. plenty of time for u to get back.

CHAPTER 21

NAN AND ANGIE PLAN

Two glasses of wine and I practically attacked Charlie in the parking lot last night. At least it was behind the restaurant where nobody could see us.

Angie was a little embarrassed at the memory of turning his comforting goodnight hug into an exchange of fiery kisses and caressing. Although she wouldn't deny it was good.

He was willing to give me the time and space I need to figure things out without any pressure or ultimatums. That's all it took. What is wrong with me? I'm so damn confused!

At seven in the morning, she wasn't out of bed yet. *It's way past time for coffee.*

Less penitent after two cups of coffee and a foamy shower, she decided what she did wasn't so awful. After all, Charlie was an old friend and they enjoyed each other's company. Ben had just come into her life. She owed him nothing.

Then she remembered what it was like when they were together. He made her wild with desire, and she loved it when they satisfied each other without inhibitions. She never felt like that, before she met him, or after he left.

In the middle of getting ready for work, Angie decided to play hooky. She remembered the few other times she was too distracted to work. They were when Ben left, after she had to have the Vet put her old cat, Bingo, to sleep, and when her husband died.

"Hi," Angie told the answering service. "I'm working from home today. Tell them I'm available if they need me. I'll call in later." She texted her office manager saying she was fine, but wanted to spend some time with an old friend. *At least that part is true.*

I need to talk to someone who won't tell me I'm crazy or promiscuous, or both.

She hit speed dial on her phone. After four rings, a machine answered. "Hey, Nan, pick up. It's Angie."

A cranky voice answered. "Yeah. I know it's you. It's seven-thirty in the morning too. Whathahell is so important?"

"I'll tell you if you have breakfast with me. My treat, someplace nice."

"Sure. Jim's gone to an early meeting and I'm just up. Haven't started painting yet. Hey! You saw Charlie last night! Is this about that?"

"Sort of. But I need your help with some other things too. Vianni's in three quarters of an hour? I'm in jeans and a sweatshirt. OK?"

"Wait, Angie. You mean you're not going to work?"

"No. I'm not. I'll make a mess of anything I touch."

"Hon, it's not like you to do this. Seriously, are you OK?" Nan sounded fully awake and concerned. "You want me to come over there?"

121

"No. I need to get myself out of this house. If not, I'll sit and stew."

"Fine. I'm heading for the shower."

Forty-five minutes later, the two women were looking at plates of sinful pancakes, bacon, mounds of butter, jugs of syrup, and a pot of coffee on their table. Angie had ordered without consulting Nan.

"Geez, Angie, what is worth this food orgy?"

"Nan, I almost had another kind of orgy with Charlie last night."

Her friend's forkful of moist pancake stopped halfway to her mouth.

"Huh? What'd he do to turn you on that much? And what does the 'almost' mean?"

"OK, I was nervous telling him about Ben. I started to cry, but he was a sweetheart about it. Fed me everything I like and another glass of wine. Then he walked me out to my car, hugged me, and didn't even try his usual massage." Her face was pink with embarrassment. "He was the one who stopped us from doing more and told me everything would be OK. It's the first time I've ever thought of him as gallant."

The smile on Nan's face was sympathetic. She reached over and put her hand over Angie's. "You made out with him because you felt grateful, guilty, relieved and maybe a little horny, right?"

"Yes. I'm wondering if I'm going crazy. I think Charlie might be ready for monogamy. I could never be with more than one man at once. I know it's old fashioned, but that's how I am. Then Ben showed up. We kissed after breakfast Tuesday. I thought I'd melt when he touched me. I'm thinking I'll go further. I just don't know how much or when."

"Oh for heaven's sake, Angie. What's the big deal? You're an uncommitted single woman, at least for now. Good for you. I hope you'll make out with Ben, or do more, if that's what you want. Don't worry about Charlie. Yeah, I think he does care about you, but he loves the chase. There are no guarantees for a future with him. You two could make it work together, but do you want to settle, when you're not sure? If you were convinced Charlie was the one, you wouldn't have agreed to see Ben. I think you're finally putting yourself first for a change." Nan continued. "You're not crazy, and there's nothing wrong about anything you've done."

Angie nodded and her face lost its tightness. "Oh Nan. You've made me feel so much better."

"That's what best friends do. Are you and Ben still on for tomorrow night?"

"Yeah. And that's the other reason I need your help."

"All you have to do is ask."

"Could you get me into your spa for a wax today or tomorrow? The kind you were telling me about? "

Nan didn't even try to suppress a lascivious smile. "You mean a full leg and bikini wax?"

"I guess. And a mani and pedi? I just got a haircut and color. I've let the other stuff go for a while."

"Angie, you are in luck. I had my own maintenance work scheduled for this afternoon. If I can't get you an appointment, you can have mine. No problem. I get everything done before it's an emergency. I can wait."

A few minutes on the phone was all it took. Angie had an appointment with Nan's beauty team.

Over fresh coffee, they continued to discuss the date with Ben.

"What're you going to wear tomorrow night?"

"It's a casual date, so I thought a silk blouse under a velour top with slacks and booties."

"Soft, touchable fabrics, but modest. I like it. Too early for deep vees and lots of leg."

"Nan!"

"Just thinkin' ahead. You got some pretty sleep stuff? Even if they were made of rabbit fur with cutouts those size triple X tee shirts wouldn't cut it."

Angie burst out laughing. "I do have some lacy nighties and lingerie if there's an occasion that calls for them."

After another half-hour, they hugged goodbye.

"We'll talk Saturday morning. I'll want details," Nan told her friend.

The rest of the day passed quickly for Angie. She felt pretty and sexy after her afternoon at the spa. Nobody needed her at the office. In a calmer mood, she spent the evening cleaning up some work files.

Jake called to check in because she left late and was home early. She told him everything was fine, but it was going to be an early night for her.

Just before falling asleep, Angie's last thought was, *I don't want to settle for sensible and OK this time. I want something wonderful.*

CHAPTER 22

FIRST DATE

I'm *seeing Ben tonight. Oh yeah!* Angie was awake before her alarm sounded. It was five-thirty in the morning and still dark out. She was too excited to go back to sleep. After several long stretches, she just lay there, trying to relax.

I need to calm down. This won't be a big deal. He said we're having a casual date. We could be going bowling for all I know. Geez. That'd be strange. Nah. We'll probably do something classier than that. Won't we? What's casual anyway?

OK. Time to quit lying here going crazy. Coffee will help. Maybe a little early morning walk will settle me down. No. Coffee and the early news. I don't feel like walking. But I should.

She compromised and spent a half-hour on her treadmill.

After a warm shower with lavender soap, she padded barefoot down to the kitchen. That pearly red color looked good on her toes. The waxed parts of her had stopped stinging overnight too. *Haven't had that kind of wax job done in years.* Angie refused to let herself think about why she decided to groom herself so carefully now.

Only the little porch light was on in Jake's house across the street. That meant he was at Eileen's. He was so happy about her moving in full time, and she was radiant the other night.

Wonder if I'll ever be that happy? I was when I was with Ben.

She argued with herself. *Dan was a good man. Yeah, but was it like with Ben? No, it wasn't. Nothing could ever be that good. Dan and I had a calm and comfortable life together. It was mostly fine. I need to keep in mind what Ben did. He dumped me. But, that was twenty-four years ago. People change. Do they really?*

"Stop!" She said aloud. "Just stop. It's a date. You're not making any commitment. Have fun. And stop talking to yourself."

Angie threw on a raincoat and retrieved the paper from the front walk.

She poured the hot, aromatic coffee into one of her favorite English Bone China mugs and carried it, along with the paper, into the den. Stretched on the couch, cup on the coffee table, she opened the paper.

The stories didn't hold her attention. She flipped on the TV. Her favorite weatherman assured her the evening would be clear, crisp and colder than normal. That would be perfect for wearing her new brown leather bomber jacket over the silk blouse and the velour top.

She couldn't stop thinking about tonight. *I'd love to find out a lot more about his life. His business card had numbers for London and Naples Florida. What's the deal with that? Well, I can't interrogate him. At least not yet.* She wouldn't let herself wonder if he was still a world-class lover. After all, what would that have to do with a first date?

Angie dozed a bit after the warm coffee, waking up again at seven-thirty. She checked her email and was delighted to see one from Ben. Didn't he have her cell for texting?

"Good morning, Angela. Casablanca is at the Lincoln Theater in Beverly. Would you like to go to an early show at 6:30 and have some dinner after? The Plover Cove Tavern is nice. I could pick you up at quarter to 6. Later, B."

Leave it to Ben to remember how much I love that movie! It's so damn romantic and sad though. What the hell. It's appropriate. We were romantic too, back in the day. And we certainly had a sad ending.

She answered,

"Perfect! Looking forward. A."

Did I give him my street address? Probably. How else would he know where to pick me up?

The day went by fast. As soon as Angie got to the office, she concentrated on work. Friday morning was reserved for a staff meeting to review client issues and care plans. There was one person designated to handle emergencies that tended to happen as the weekend approached.

The nurses used the afternoon for check-in calls to clients just to say hello and see how things were going. She worked on a newspaper article.

Only the weekend On-Call person stayed later on Friday, to be sure all information was current in the secure laptop. Angie told everyone she was off the grid for the next couple of days. Her two long-term clients were aware that another RN, whom they had met, would be available if anything came up. Both were stable, so she felt comfortable with being away. Jake had her cell number. Eileen was going to be with him all weekend, so he most likely wouldn't call.

Angie knew she wasn't indispensable, but work had been her savior during the hard times. Sometimes she used it as an excuse to avoid things she just didn't want to do. Maybe it was time to rethink that.

By four-thirty, she was home with plenty of time to get ready. Her clothes were hanging, lacy undies were on the bed, and she could have a relaxing cup of tea.

As the kettle whistled, Angie thought she saw a little wetness on the floor by the cabinet under the sink.

Must've spilled something this morning. No, it seems to be seeping out.

She opened the door to find everything wet, including the bottom of the cabinet. There was a small stream of water along the pipe.

Oh, crap. Something must have loosened. Just the thing for my new manicure. Those French white tips can chip so easily.

She went to the garage for an adjustable wrench. Dan was never good at fixing little things around the house, and Angie enjoyed fiddling with minor repairs. She found the wrench, grabbed heavy rubber gloves, got a box to stow all of the stuff from under the sink, and headed back to the kitchen.

So much for tea. Geez. It's quarter to five. He'll be here in an hour.

After ten minutes of fiddling, she couldn't get the strapping off around the pipe. The leak seemed to be getting worse.

Damn! I can't do this. Wonder if Jake is home?

He picked up on the second ring. "Hey, aren't you goin' out with your friend tonight? What's up?"

She told him about the leak, that she couldn't fix it, and she didn't want to look awful with chipped nails when Ben arrived.

"Leave, it, Honey. I'm on my way. It'll be fine. If I need anything, Billy at the hardware place'll have it. Go get ready right now."

Angie thanked god for her wonderful friend and dashed upstairs with a bottle of cold sparkling water. *I only have a half-hour. I'm sweating, and my hair's a mess.*

Another shower, with a spritz of Chanel in several spots calmed her down. That, and the sound of Jake clattering around in the kitchen. Fifteen minutes would be time enough for light makeup and getting dressed.

Is that the doorbell? He's not due yet.

She heard Jake greeting Ben. Oh well. It was what it was. She went back to finishing her make-up.

At the sound of the bell, Jake wiped his hands and headed for the door, wrench in hand. He was delighted to have a chance to give this guy the once-over. He prided himself on sizing people up fast. *I hope he's what she wants.*

Jake opened the heavy door and greeted the visitor pleasantly. "Hello. Angie will be down in a minute. A pipe under the sink sprung a leak about an hour ago, and, instead of calling me, she tried to fix it herself. C'mon in. I'm Jake. Live across the street."

Ben stepped into a large foyer. He felt instantly comfortable. Light colors were punctuated with touches of red in some pictures. Hardwood floors shone.

Jake continued as he shepherded the visitor into the living room. "Sorry I can't offer to shake hands. Mine are a little greasy. Moving that nut was a bitch!"

"No worries. I'm Ben Whitcomb, an old friend of Angela's." He introduced himself with a smile, meeting

Jake's eyes directly. "Recently moved to the area. Camping out over in Plover Cove for the moment."

Jake liked his manner and unruffled reaction to what was happening.

"You say she tried to fix it herself?" Ben asked, peering into the organized chaos of the floor in front of the open cabinet. He followed Jake into the kitchen. "Anything I can do? I've fixed a lot of sinks and toilets myself. They always seem to need attention at inconvenient times."

"Nah, almost done. Grab a seat at the counter."

Jake resumed his position on the kitchen rug, his upper body under the sink.

"Yeah. She's pretty good with little repairs. Woman's damned independent. Doesn't want to bother people by asking for help. Was upset this time though. Said something about not wanting to mess up her nails. Wanting to look good."

"Jake! Are you giving away all of my secrets?"

He slid out from under the cabinet. "Nah, Honey. We were just gettin' acquainted."

Ben was on his feet, beaming. "Well, Angela, you certainly do look good!"

Jake was watching them, as he pretended to clean up the area.

He saw Angie walk over and take both of Ben's hands in her own. He towered over her five feet-eight inches. Jake couldn't remember her ever looking that happy. Ben bent down and gave her a light kiss on her cheek. She didn't seem to mind that at all.

"Hey, you kids run along. I'll finish here, maybe have one of those fancy beers you keep for me, Angie, and lock up. Have a good time."

He turned directly to Ben. "Next time you're around, drop over for a drink. I pour a mean single malt. Nice to meet you."

"Thanks Jake, I'll take you up on that. Very nice to meet you as well. And to find out about Angela's hidden talents."

Jake was relieved. This Ben seemed OK. Angie was obviously attracted to him, and he definitely acted as if he felt the same way. "I'd love to see her with someone as good as she deserves," Jake told the fridge as he found a bottle of Harp.

CHAPTER 23
AT THE MOVIE

Ben gave Angie a hand onto the high seat of his Land Rover, and chuckled about the start of their first formal date in twenty-four years. He settled behind the wheel, turning toward her with a curious look. "So, do you run a little home repair service among your other ventures? Except, of course, when you're unavailable because of a fresh manicure?"

"Blast Jake for telling you I was upset about that." She laughed at her old friend's willingness to reveal her worry over something that must seem so trivial to a man. "It's just that I didn't want to look scruffy. Really, I'm not all that handy, just good at tightening nuts and bolts here and there."

He smiled, leaned over and took her left hand, pretending to examine her nails carefully. "Well, Angela, you definitely do not look scruffy. Most of the men who see us tonight will consider me a lucky fellow."

His comment made her feel surprisingly happy. "Thank you for the kind words, Sir. Now, if we're going to get to the movie on time, we'd better get going. You'll probably need both hands to drive, won't you?" She smiled at him, looking straight into his eyes as she gently withdrew her hand and moved slightly away.

There was some traffic, even with the shortcut through Salem. They chatted easily. "You've known Jake a long time, have you?"

"Oh, Ben, I love that man. He was there when we moved in. At first, I wasn't working, so we got to know each other when we were out gardening or walking. We hit it off right away."

Ben glanced over. He enjoyed hearing how she felt about the old man.

"Later, after," she stopped for a minute, clenched her fists, then continued, "after Dan died, Jake appointed himself my guardian angel. He made life a lot easier. We became quite close."

Ben wanted to give her a minute. He thought she choked up a little when she mentioned her husband's death.

"He told me he lives across the street. Also hinted that you might be a bit more independent than you had to be."

She leaned as close to Ben as her seat belt would allow. "Jake should talk! He'll only ask for help if he's at death's door."

"Well, he looks like he's in great shape, so someone's looking after him. How old is he? Maybe in his early seventies?"

Angie laughed. "Jake had his eightieth birthday bash a couple of months ago. He actually has two people to keep him on track. He and I keep an eye on each other, but Eileen, the love of his life, keeps him happy and healthy."

"Good for Jake! He seems to be a great guy."

Moreover, I could tell that he was deciding what kind of person I might be at this stage of my life. You must have told him our story. I'm glad you have Jake. Even if he would rip my heart out with a claw hammer if he thought I'd ever hurt you.

"We're close to the theater, Ben." She tapped his arm. "Parking is at the next left. Just in time, too. It's 6:15."

He noticed she waited for him to come around and open her door. *A modern independent woman, who still enjoys old-fashioned courtesy. Nice.*

Comfortable after the easy conversation in the car, she stood aside and let him get their tickets and select seats. Ben needed one on the aisle because he couldn't fold himself into a regular space.

Angie never tired of *Casablanca's* dramatic opening, where Ugarte, one of the shady characters, begged to be saved from the enemy. She sat up in her chair, leaned forward, and grabbed the arm of her seat. Ben enjoyed watching her react. He put his hand lightly over hers for reassurance. Much to his delight, she grabbed it in a tight grip and moved her body closer to him.

Love this movie, the more tense, the better, was Ben's reaction.

As the story continued, Bogart played his tough-guy-with-a-conscience role to perfection. The backdrop was Casablanca, 1942, at the beginning of WW II with spies everywhere. Angie kept holding Ben's hand, engrossed in the story.

Ben smiled, glancing at her expressive face. *Wonder if she even realizes what she's doing?*

His hand feels so good. I've wanted to touch him since I saw him this evening. Glad the action gives me an excuse. Wish I could sit even closer. Can't believe how he makes me feel. She wasn't thinking about Charlie at all.

Although she knew the story by heart, Angie teared up at the parts where Rick's long lost love, Ilsa, came back into his life only to be noble and remain with her heroic husband.

Maybe it's not the movie that's making me so sad. She let go of Ben's hand and sat back.

Don't know what she's remembering, but I can't let her withdraw from me. He slipped his long arm over the back of her seat and let his fingers cup very lightly around her shoulder. *Oh, that soft top feels good. I've got to hold my hand very still. I want to comfort her. Not good if she thinks I'm pushing.*

Angie shivered just slightly at his touch. *Damn! I can't believe how much I want him. In the three years I've been single I haven't felt this way. This is crazy.* She nestled her shoulder into his hand. He had to work hard not to change his light touch into a caress.

After the bittersweet ending, they both sat for a minute when the lights came on. Ben stood and helped her with her jacket, being careful to touch only her shoulders. Angela's eyes were bright, and he didn't think it was from lingering tears over the movie.

A brisk wind was blowing when they left the theater.

"BRRRR! Ben it's gotten really cold!"

"Yes, indeed it has. Good thing we're parked nearby. Here, I'm used to damp and cold weather. Let's use this to keep you warm."

He slipped his heavy suede jacket over her leather one. It reached to below her knees.

"You'll freeze!"

"Not if we move along, I won't. Let's go."

They trotted to the car, holding hands. He opened the door, and, before getting in, she reached up to drape the jacket on his shoulders. It took a minute for Angie to realize she had both arms around Ben, with her head just below his chin.

"What a nice way to thank me!" Ben turned her position into the opportunity for a quick hug and brushed the top of her head with a kiss. Angie gave him a playful push away.

"Start the engine and get some heat on, please. Or else I'll need to drink lots of brandy to get rid of this chill." *Although brandy isn't the only thing that would get me warmer. Much warmer.*

Ben smiled at her comment. He didn't think it would be prudent to say he'd like to try other ways to make her chill disappear.

They sparred good-naturedly about the film on the way to dinner.

"So Ben, what do you think would have happened if Rick and Ilsa ended up together?"

"Well, let's see. They met and fell in love in the middle of a war. Quite a bit of drama there. They met for the second time in a hotbed of intrigue. More drama. They'd probably be bored to death with each other in weeks once there was no danger to add spice to things."

She turned toward him, looking horrified at the thought. "Well, you're certainly not a romantic! I've been in love with Bogart for years. Who could ever get tired of those basset hound eyes and that all-knowing face?"

They pulled into the tavern parking lot. He parked the car, and faced her with the corners of his mouth turned down.

"Angela, does your taste run to short, sad men with sketchy pasts? Do I even stand a chance with my happy disposition, unblemished reputation, and over-tall stature?"

Angie didn't answer immediately. She sat very still, looking at him with her warm brown eyes wide and unwavering. He stopped talking as well and returned her look.

"I think you might have a tiny chance, Ben," she said softly.

He took her manicured hand in his, and kissed it, answering, "I'd like that."

Without lingering longer, he hurried them out of the car. The way he was feeling, if he didn't break the mood he'd have to kiss her and it wouldn't be a quick light kiss this time. However, he wasn't sure if Angela was ready for that and he couldn't afford to make her uncomfortable in any way. He'd have to wait.

CHAPTER 24

GETTING WARMER

B en put his arm around Angie's waist on the way from the Land Rover to the Tavern. "So you won't blow away in this ocean wind," he told her.

They welcomed the warmth inside. "Would you like to sit upstairs in the Crow's Nest, Ben? It's away from the bar and not so noisy." *We're less likely to run into anyone I know up there too. Charlie and I have been here several times. I don't want anybody reporting to him about tonight.*

"Sounds good, Angela. Is there a nice view?"

"It should be spectacular on a night this clear."

Their circular booth faced floor to ceiling windows showcasing the foamy harbor wavelets as they broke on the shore. Autumn stars reflected on the almost black water.

"You found a perfect spot for us to start getting reacquainted, Angela." He resisted the urge to take her hand. She wondered why this place suddenly seemed romantic. *Careful there, lady. This is not twenty-five years ago. He's nearly a stranger. Remember, slow.*

Deciding on food and ordering drinks kept the conversation flowing. Ben asked for a single malt, MacCallan's this time. Angie wanted her usual Pinot Grigio with ice on the side. They both had crab cakes and the Tavern's special Caesar Salad. Angie asked for double anchovies.

"I'd like them too," Ben told the server.

They ate with gusto, still bickering over the Casablanca lovers' possible future if they hadn't parted.

After the salad, Ben looked at her happily. "Angela! I thought nobody in the world, other than myself of course, liked anchovies. It's a sign that we're compatible on many levels."

"Well, it's a sign that we both like strongly flavored little fishes with pungent odors, anyway," she teased him. "At least we won't smell them from each other."

"Yes, and that might be important," Ben commented innocently. She reached for one last scrap of anchovy, pretending to ignore him.

They talked about a variety of subjects, and two hours flew by. Ben dipped a toe into the past. "We've developed many of the same interests over the years, haven't we Angela?"

She followed his lead, smiling when she answered, "Well, I'm not surprised. We liked the same things back when."

He changed the subject. *This is like a first date. Not the time for serious talk. We're connecting now. Let's just enjoy that.*

"How about an Irish Coffee to get us warmed up for the cold ride home?" he suggested. "I've heard they make good ones here."

Before her brain kicked in to control her mouth, she heard herself saying, "Mine are probably better. Why not let me make us some?"

He gratefully accepted, flagged down the waiter immediately, and got them out of there in minutes. She noted how quickly he managed that and chuckled to herself.

I may not have made that offer completely unconsciously. Well, I did it, so we'll see what happens.

"It's very gracious of you to do this, Angela," Ben remarked on the short drive to her house.

She smiled. "Well, I hope you'll be happy with my bartending."

Oh, I'll be happy. You can be sure of that.

They went into Angie's kitchen, which Jake had left spotless. "It's cleaner than it's been all week. I'm afraid neatness is not my greatest virtue, Ben."

"Hmmm. And would you like to discuss some of your other bad habits?" he asked suggestively, perching on the edge of a counter stool.

"Not now. I promised you a special treat. Can you make coffee while I do the clotted cream?"

"Of course I can make coffee. Where do you keep it? I see the machine." He was heading toward the cabinets.

"Second canister on the left counter. Scooper's in there. Use three flat scoops and fill the carafe to the six cup level. Run the water to get it good and cold, please."

"Yes, Ma'am. As you order." Ben was completing his task while watching Angie move efficiently around the kitchen. He admired her taste. Burnished cherry cabinets hung above a white stone counter. She didn't have the usual stainless appliances, but white ones instead. The floor was a light gray-green tile. He liked the ambiance.

Coffee perfume filled the kitchen. Angie had Jameson's whiskey and a bowl of cream, whipped to a perfect clotted consistency, on the table. Large glasses with green shamrocks on them, silver spoons, and a bowl of sugar sat on a tray. She added some biscotti covered in dark chocolate.

The two of them bustling around in the kitchen took away any awkwardness about being together in her home.

"These glasses are made for hot coffee," Angie said, "so why don't you pour? I'll add the sugar, whiskey and cream. Shall we drink it in the living room?"

Ben carried the tray and set it on a low table in front of a comfortable looking couch. She flicked on the gas fireplace.

Seated on the couch, she motioned him to join her. He was surprised at how easily they had slipped into such a companionable mode, but glad that they had.

"Hey, you do make an excellent Irish Coffee!"

"I had a good teacher. Dan didn't drink much, but he loved one of these on a cold night. I'm lucky. Coffee doesn't bother me at any time, so I can have one late and still sleep well."

"Angela, you'll need to teach me your technique. I am known for my Scotch selection, and I'm talented with most any kind of gin. But I need to drink these more often."

She smiled. "This was a lovely evening, Ben."

"Yes. And I'm looking forward to Sunday. Would a trip to the Berkshires suit you? We could have brunch on the way out, explore a few museums, see the foliage, and have dinner on the way back. It'd be a whole day, but we can take breaks from each other if you get tired of me."

She gave a low, throaty laugh. "I do not remember your being so accommodating." *Oh no! I am way too off guard. I didn't want to bring up anything from the past! How will he react?*

"Nor do I remember you being so snippy, Miss," Ben said as he moved toward her with a soft smile. "But I do remember some other things."

He reached out, took the glass very carefully from her hand and set it on the table. Then he moved closer, slowly, giving her time to move away if she wanted to.

Angie welcomed his kiss, amazed at what she was feeling. They hugged each other tightly, and he nuzzled her neck. *I haven't felt like this forever.* She lifted her head, met his eyes, and kissed him again with a passion that surprised them both. His tongue gently pushed at her teeth. The tip touched hers. She whimpered softly in response. There was no denying how they felt.

After another long kiss, Angie pulled back slightly. Ben didn't try to stop her.

"Well, look at us. What happened to taking this slowly?"

"I think we forgot," he teased, releasing her from his arms and taking her hand lightly.

"Ben, I'm kind of old fashioned about these things." She picked up her cold Irish coffee and took a sip. "I, well, I'm a little shy about sharing men with other ladies. Not that I have any right to..."

He put his finger over her lips. "Angela, I told you at breakfast that there have been a few women..."

"Ben, of course..."

"Shhh let me finish." He was at the end of the couch now. "I haven't been intimate with anyone in about a year. I was sorting some things out. You and I are certainly attracted to each other. However, you're right about not rushing. So, let's do turns. I started kissing you tonight. You take the lead next time." He looked gleefully satisfied with himself as he got up from the couch.

She could feel herself blushing. "Ben! I'm not sure if I can come right out and do that."

He smiled. "I will take broad hints, my love. But you will have to make your intentions quite clear." He tried to sound like a stern schoolmaster. She stood, and he put his arms around her lightly.

She managed to sound demure. "You drive a hard bargain, Ben, but I'll try to live with it. What time Sunday?"

"Nine OK?" He grabbed his jacket from the corner of the chair where he had tossed it and walked toward the door.

"I'm going to give you a kiss on the cheek right now. Any further move is yours."

She returned the chaste kiss. However, his hug was tight enough to leave no doubt how he felt about her.

When he left, she was exhausted and excited at the same time. Ben rekindled a passion she thought was dead long ago. After putting their glasses into the dishwasher and eating the last soft biscotti, she went to bed. Her thoughts cascaded, making sleep impossible.

I wanted to tear off his clothes, and mine too! Why didn't I? Because I got scared. I didn't want him to know he could still make me feel that way either. There's a good chance this won't amount to anything. I might lose Charlie over a foolish fling. Odd though, I didn't think of him once tonight. All I could think of was how wonderful I felt.

After an hour, she finally fell asleep, still aroused, and wishing for Ben's arms around her.

CHAPTER 25

THE TRAP

On the short drive home, all Ben could think about was Angela and how she made him feel. *I was like a horny kid. At my age, self-control shouldn't be a challenge.*

He'd wanted to kiss her all night, from the time she accidentally wrapped her arms around him after the movie, trying to give his coat back. He resisted the impulse though, sensing it might make her uncomfortable.

Later, after they made the drinks and got comfortable in front of the fire, he couldn't hold off any longer. The memory of how pretty and happy she looked as she teased him about how he had become accommodating made him smile.

She's smart, funny, considerate and beautiful. It's not just a physical attraction we have, either. There's a deeper connection and I don't think it's just the memory of when we were together. I hope she feels it too.

Ben knew he couldn't sleep. He decided to change and hit the condo gym for a while. *Maybe I can work off some of this tension.*

On the way into the garage, he saw Ollie's unit had lights on in several rooms. *I know I didn't leave it like that. Can't be burglars, they'd use flashlights. Maybe there was a leak, or a fire or something and someone called Emergency Services. That's all I need. I'm supposed to catch a one o'clock plane to meet her in New York for a late lunch. Wasn't going to be an easy talk anyhow, but if her condo is trashed, it'll be a helluva lot harder.*

He parked the Range Rover and ran up the two flights of stairs from the garage. Ollie's door was closed and looked fine. *If there had been a problem, someone would probably have left a note.* Puzzled, he tried it, and found he needed a key. When he did slip in, very quietly, he saw a red alligator overnight case on the living room floor. A light fur jacket was flung across the back of the white couch. Ollie's scent floated in the air. He heard the shower running.

Ben crept into the guest room, grabbed his laptop with a few file folders, and left as quickly and silently as he arrived. The shower sounds stopped just as he closed the door. His adrenalin was pumping as if he just finished a hard workout.

Goddamit! Ollie said she was doing a Sunday afternoon seminar in New York. Probably planning to stay overnight and fly back tomorrow. Unless something happened and she's home for good. Whatever's going on, she wanted to surprise me.

He was annoyed. Angela didn't know he was housesitting for a friend who just happened to be an ex-lover. *I was going to clear that up Sunday. Didn't think it was a conversation for our first date in decades. What a mess!*

At one in the morning, parked along the beach in his Land Rover, he called the Washington Hotel in Salem. Between Halloween and the foliage, he was sure they'd be fully booked. Luckily, there was a vacancy if he'd take a junior suite.

I'd sleep on a couch in the lobby if I had to. No way am I staying in the same condo with Ollie. If I know her, she has the champagne chilling, and is wearing the most seductive thing she owns. The woman doesn't give up!

He stopped at an all-night drug store to pick up a toothbrush, toothpaste, a disposable razor and shaving cream. He hoped the hotel room had a mini bar. Ben needed a drink.

At check-in, the night manager was courteous and efficient. There was no unnecessary chatter. Ben was on the elevator to his room within ten minutes from the time he arrived.

The Scotch from the minibar wasn't bad. He sipped it with only a drop of water. Maybe it would let him get a few hours' sleep.

I don't want to barge in on Ryan, or Pete and Nellie over the weekend. I'll tell them, if Ollie calls, to say that I stayed there. He sent a text to each of his sons.

Need your help. If Ollie calls, I slept there tonight. Will explain. All good.

His cell shrilled in the quiet room. "Dunk," it was Ryan. "What's going on? You OK?"

"Yeah. Fine. Ollie showed up at the condo while I was out. She wants something that's not going to work. I can't be in her place if she's there. I'll fill you guys in when we go to sign the papers on Tuesday. Cover for me?"

Ryan roared laughing. "Dunk, never thought you'd be asking that! Sure. You were here. I'll tell Pete in the morning. Night."

Ben fell asleep around two. He got a text from Ollie saying she was in town for the weekend. He'd answer it in the morning. They'd have dinner in Cambridge or Boston tomorrow. *Someone'd be sure to see us if we went out around here, and Angela would probably know about it before we got to dessert.*

⊶⊷

OLLIE

Ollie was not happy. *Where the hell is he? Nothing's open around here after one in the morning. I knew he had something going when he was so shy last week.*

She was on her second glass of champagne. Things weren't going as planned.

OK, so I didn't call ahead. I think it was damn nice of me to come here instead of making him come to New York. He said we needed to talk. Easier to talk here than in a restaurant.

"Oh. Oh. Unless he didn't want privacy. He wanted us in public. He thought I wouldn't give him any trouble that way." She heard herself shouting.

He's probably out with someone else. He could be in Cambridge though. Plans to move there in a few weeks anyway. Stuff's still in his room. Wonder why he took the guest room? Master's bigger. Can't call the boys, he'd be pissed out of his mind. Well, it's one-thirty. I'll try texting.

Ollie tied the belt of her royal blue satin negligee. She had left it open, to expose the lace of her matching gown. It barely covered her full breasts. She poured herself another glass of champagne.

What a waste of a five-hundred dollar outfit. He always loved nice lingerie. Said it was like wrapping paper on a special present.

Taking it off added to the fun. Must give the guy credit. He knows how to make a woman happy!

The text was short.

Kno it's late. Need to talk before u lv for NY. Dinner still on but plan chng will make it easier. XXX.

She fell asleep on the sofa without an answer.

CHAPTER 26

CHARLIE COMPETES

The doorbell chimed. It interrupted Angie's dream where Ben started to kiss her.

It has to be a package or something. They'll leave it. She turned over, pulled up the blankets and hoped the dream would start where it left off. The chimes continued in bursts, along with loud knocking on the door.

She looked at the clock. It was nine. *I never sleep that late! Who's down there?* More chimes ringing, louder knocking.

OK, OK. She threw on a pair of flannel pants and ran down the stairs. *Whoever it is must have something important. They've been making a racket for at least five minutes.*

"Mornin' Angie." It was Bob Craigan from Rock Harbor Posies. He was carrying a multistem yellow orchid plant in a white container painted with a delicate Chinese pattern. The plant had mature flowers and little buds scattered on the five stems.

Angie gasped. "Bob, that is one of the most beautiful orchids I've ever seen! The pot is gorgeous too." She stood on the porch, looking doubtful that the delivery was really for her.

"Yep. Jeannie told me I had to bring this over myself. Said not to dare leave it on the porch or give it to a neighbor. That's why I kept ringin' the bell and bangin' on your door."

"Well, I appreciate that, Bob."

Still holding the plant closely, he continued to chat. "Yep. Had to be special-ordered. Took a while. Jeannie said it cost a fortune but the English guy said not to worry. Covered the tip for delivery too."

Angie couldn't stop a burst of laughter. However, she was beginning to get chilly. The oversize tee and flannels were no match for the very cold morning.

"Oops. Don't think I was s'posed to tell you that last part."

"It's OK Bob. I won't tell your wife." She held her arms out for the plant.

"You sure do get a lot of flowers. All those roses from Charlie last week, now this. You're a popular lady." There was curiosity in his voice.

"Bye, Bob. Thanks again." She wanted to get the lovely blooms out of the chilly air.

Once inside, away from Bob's curious look, she opened the card.

"Angela, Thank you for being kind enough to see me again. Hope these are still one of your favorites. B."

She chuckled at the formality of Ben's note. *It's that British sense of propriety. He must have ordered this after breakfast Tuesday. They always have been my favorites, but only he knows that. I couldn't stand to have yellow orchids around after he left.*

She hugged herself and kissed the card. Charlie's roses were still beautiful in their vase as well. They reminded her that Nan, Jim, she and Charlie were going to have dinner tonight at the club. *I'm silly to think twice about that. Charlie still has Liliana. I've been straight with him about Ben. No reason to change the way we are as long as we're both OK with it. Give the scruples a rest, woman.*

She just started the coffee when the phone rang.

"Soooo, how was it? I waited 'til practically afternoon to call you. Didn't want to interrupt anything."

"Nan, it's nine-thirty. Let me get coffee. Hold on."

She smiled as she sneaked what had already brewed and brought it and the phone into the living room. Nan had told her she'd want details.

"Hi again."

"Don't 'hi' me! And how come you're just getting coffee? What happened to make you sleep late? Tell all!"

"It was wonderful from hello to goodnight. A very romantic goodnight." Angela snuggled into the sofa, remembering last night with Ben.

"How romantic?"

"Hot."

"Oh, for heaven's sake, Angie! Did you or didn't you?"

"No, we didn't. I just couldn't on a technical first date within a week of meeting him!"

She laughed at her friend's 'humph.'

"But, I've decided that keeping everything platonic and slow probably won't work anymore. I like Ben. A lot. We're going on our all-day date tomorrow."

"Angie, you'll need a tote anyhow with snacks and a few things. Take something nice to wear just in case you decide to stay overnight somewhere. Be sure it's slinky, with silk or lace. And wear sexy underwear."

"Way ahead of you, Nan. But it's a day trip. This morning at least, I wouldn't mind us staying overnight. I think I'm getting to be a loose woman."

"Congratulations. I'm proud of you," she was laughing with glee. "Dinner tonight should be interesting."

"Yeah. How'll I handle it when Charlie wants to come in after?"

"Got it covered. Don't worry. Gotta go. Jim and I are going for a late breakfast and then to see some foliage. See you at seven. Bye."

"Seven it is. Have fun."

Nan and Jim were still in love after thirty years of marriage. They enjoyed being with friends, but Angie knew they treasured spending time together. It gave her hope for her own future. Jim and Ben had been good friends too. They all lived in Boston back then.

About a year after Ben, the couple had dragged her to a party where she and Dan met. She wasn't crazy about him at first, but he was persistent, showered her with attention, and eventually, she fell in love with him. They married three years after Ben left. It seemed a lifetime ago.

Now it's another lifetime. What'll I do with it? Maybe it's time to take some chances.

Angie spent the afternoon doing some fall planting in her front yard. She put on heavy gloves to protect her hands, then pulled geraniums and put in winter cabbages. Working the dirt, getting fresh air, and having casual conversations with the neighbors took her mind off everything else.

Jake and Eileen were away for the weekend. They left a message saying have fun, and asking her for dinner Tuesday night. The message told her to bring her friend if she liked. Smiling at that, Angie guessed they both wanted a chance to spend some time with Ben.

It was five when she realized Charlie was picking her up in a couple of hours. A shower and taming her hair into something that wasn't a nest of wild curls would take a while. She hadn't thought much about what to wear, but was quick to find something Charlie would probably like.

Why am I fussing? Last night I was smoking hot for Ben. This morning, Nan and I were planning how I was going to get him to take me to bed. Now, I'm hedging my bets by keeping Charlie interested in case things don't work out. This isn't me. Or maybe it is. Whatever. Nothing wrong with looking good.

The black silk dress, with a boat neck and long sleeves, skimmed her figure without clinging. Large gold earrings, along with a string of lustrous pearls, made the simple outfit elegant and understated. The dress hit just above her knees, so she decided on sheer stockings with simple black sling back pumps. Just as she took a final peek in the mirror, the door chimed.

Charlie's look told her the outfit was a success the minute she opened the door. "Wow! You ought to wear black more often, Sweetheart."

With that creamy skin and curly red hair, you are spectacular. Don't care if you need to get that Brit out of your system. I am a very understanding guy. Just so I win.

"Charlie, you always make me feel so good!"

He moved quickly to give her a close hug and a long kiss. "A down payment for later, Gorgeous." She felt guilty about enthusiastically returning the kiss, but after all, she didn't want to hurt him.

Then she pulled away quickly, not meeting his eyes.

"Angie. I know you're working things out in your head. It's OK. I won't push."

She got her coat from the closet, and turned to him again. "You're not making things easy, Charlie."

"Good." *I want to make it very hard for that Brit Bastard.*

They arrived just as Nan and Jim were seated. Nan's yellow wool suit complemented her tall and lean figure. Her black hair, newly cut to chin length, was tucked behind her ears. Huge topaz earrings were her only jewelry, except for the diamond and wedding band on her left hand. The men knew they were with two of the most stunning looking women at the club.

When the waiter arrived to take drink orders, Angie and Nan decided to split a bottle of white wine. The men had Bourbon. "To good friends, good health, and smart decisions," Charlie toasted. Neither Angie nor Nan missed the inference. Jim covered it nicely.

"Appropriate words, Charlie. Nan got a commission to paint a seascape today. Another gallery has asked her to show her work as well. Those are good decisions on the part of her new clients."

After spending some time chatting about the local happenings and town gossip, they decided on dinner, ordering clam chowder to start. The club recipe had won too many competitions to count. All four usually ate healthy foods, but the men decided tonight could be a splurge. Jim and Charlie ordered steaks. Nan and Angie had grilled salmon.

They talked more about Nan's growing success as an artist. Angie said, "I remember when you were afraid to paint because you convinced yourself nothing you did was any good."

Nan responded, "You should talk about lacking confidence. Remember how you were sure there was no market for Nurse Concierges? Now you write articles and consult all over the country."

Jim chimed in, "We're lucky these gorgeous and talented ladies put up with us, Charlie. Bet there are lots of guys who'd like to be in our shoes." He looked at his wife admiringly.

"Not telling me anything I don't know, Jim. I'd fight pretty hard to keep that from happening." There was a tinge of combativeness in Charlie's voice, covered skillfully with a huge smile and a quick hug for Angie.

Nan and Angie exchanged quick glances. Jim pretended he hadn't noticed. After dinner, the couples danced and mingled with the crowd for a while.

"Anyone want dessert?" Jim asked.

"No, Hon," Nan answered, "What I would love is one of Angie's special Irish Coffees."

"Hey, that sounds good!"

"OK. I'd love to have you all back for one."

Charlie saw his plans for a long goodnight fading. *Well, this is a chance to be the great guy. Not a total loss.*

The four drank their coffee, sitting in her living room, laughing and talking. They munched on little ice cream bon-bons for a light dessert.

At about eleven, Nan said they ought to let Angie get some sleep, and Charlie found himself caught up in the goodnights. He did manage to sneak in another kiss, but not the kind he wanted.

Angie shut off the lights quickly, leaving clean-up for the morning. Charlie wouldn't come back if he thought she had gone to sleep early.

She was excited about spending the next day with Ben. Memories of Charlie's kisses faded as she looked at the beautiful orchid in her living room.

CHAPTER 27
BEN'S PLAN

On Saturday morning, after he ran from what he was sure would have been a nasty confrontation with Ollie the night before, Ben's head was foggy. The Scotch he drank after getting settled in the hotel was punishing him.

It's eight. Hell, I was lucky to get six hours sleep. Can't believe she pulled that surprise appearance. At least I was able to grab my computer. The rest of my stuff will probably end up tossed out on the beach after we talk.

His phone pinged. It was Ollie texting.

Ben. I'm in Boston. Call ASAP. Do not get on plane.

I could tell her I took an early flight to meet some folks before dinner. No. That's too cowardly. He started shaving and told the mirror, "I'm too bloody old for this nonsense."

The second ping signaled an email from Angela.

"The orchid is too beautiful for words. I love it. Enjoyed last night so much. Looking forward to tomorrow. Warmest regards, A."

Ben was relieved at her response. He had taken a chance on appearing a little pushy by sending something so extravagant. He ordered it after their breakfast on Tuesday when he was in a celebratory mood. She probably had no idea how outrageously expensive it was. Some yellow orchids were very common. It didn't take a minute for him to respond.

"Glad it made you happy. Wonderful being with you last evening. See you at nine tomorrow. Even warmer regards. B."

He waited until ten-thirty to text Ollie. The plane he was supposed to take was leaving at one.

Whats up? All OK? Just leaving for airpt.

She answered in seconds.

In condo. Eat here? Better to talk. Where are u?

He responded fast.

Cambridge. Rather take you somewhere special. Surprise. U'll love it. Will send car for you. B ready 7.

I'm sure she'll be pissed I didn't pick her up, but I can tell her traffic is usually awful.

There was one more call he needed to make before seeing the hotel concierge to find out where he could buy fresh clothes for the next day.

Ben's old friend, Gino Morelli, owned one of the best restaurants in Boston's North End. When he first opened, Ben was starting out as a young broker. Both worked long hours, and to let off steam, they played squash together, often at midnight. It didn't take long for *Gino's* to become a success. Ben ate at the little restaurant often, and gave him a small loan for expansion. His friend never forgot the help.

They'd stayed in touch off and on over the years. Now, people had to book a table at least three weeks in advance for a Saturday night. Ben dialed a private number.

"Gino, Ben Whitcomb here."

"Ben, we haven't talked in over a year. You in town?"

"I am, and in a bit of a spot."

"With anyone I know?"

"You might. She's somewhat of a celebrity in business. I need the best place in Boston to feed her later. Then, we're going to have a, ah, delicate discussion."

"You're in luck. I have a small private dining room not in use tonight. Tell me the time."

"Seven-thirty? And Gino, I'm paying the going rate, whatever that is."

"Sure." Gino brushed him off. "We'll see you then. Can you and I have a quick drink before your guest arrives?"

"I'm having a car pick her up. I'll come around a bit early. Say quarter to seven? Thanks Gino."

After talking to Ben, Gino called to his son, who was also his business partner, "Hey, Frankie, Uncle Ben's coming in. Get a few bottles of the best red and white from the cellar. Oh, and make sure we have the Balvenie 21 ready."

"Sure, Pop. It's been forever since I've seen him."

The concierge sent Ben to a good local men's store, and called ahead to be sure a selection of casual clothing would be waiting. Something more formal was in order for dinner tonight, but that was covered. There was a custom-made charcoal suit from Bond Street at the Cambridge house. Ollie would like that. He wasn't going back to the condo to get anything, just in case she was hanging around waiting to corner him.

The emergency shopping trip was successful. He managed to find corduroy pants, a shirt, and a heavy sweater along with some underwear. Everything cost a fortune, but the service was worth it. The store promised to tailor the pants and deliver them to the hotel by three in the afternoon.

On the road to Cambridge by three-thirty, he thought about how much life could change in a week.

Ryan and Pete will give me all kinds of grief about asking them to cover for me last night. It's too soon to tell them about Angela. I'll just say a lot of things are happening. They like Ollie. No problem with them staying in touch if they want to.

She was the one who wanted freedom to, how did she put it? 'Explore options.' That was a couple of years ago. We've been just friends for a long while now. Wonder why she's so hell-bent on changing things again? She knows exactly how to get to me, and she can be almost impossible to resist. I would have stayed with her last Saturday after the game, if I hadn't met Angela. I was almost ready, and she knew it.

Well, I damn well did meet Angela, and it changed things. Last night made me realize I never completely forgot her. Ollie needs to understand that the romantic part of our relationship is finished.

He hoped there wouldn't be a scene. She loved drama. More than once she'd started a shouting match or stormed out of a restaurant in tears over some silly thing he said or didn't say.

Thank the lord Gino has a private dining room. Hope it's soundproof.

The Cambridge house was empty. He went for a run along the Charles, trying to work off the last of the Scotch-induced fog. He'd be calling a ride share to get into Boston. If he didn't have a car, he'd have an excuse to send Ollie back in a limo.

⚔

That asshole. Ollie fumed. *He's sending a car. What the hell is he up to? Maybe I just won't get into the damn car. Let him eat by himself.*

Despite her furious thoughts, she knew she'd meet Ben. They'd split before, but, never for so long.

He was ready to come back last weekend. I felt it. Then something stopped him. Maybe he wanted to be sure I wasn't just looking for casual sex. He told me he's never been into that, and made it clear he's not going to change now.

Well, I don't give up easy. It was stupid to tell him I wanted an open relationship in the first place. He doesn't get that everyone does it now. Guess it's a generational thing. He is a lot older. But he's handsome, hot, and rich. Anyway, he doesn't need to know everything I do while I travel. I'm always careful.

Ollie was stunning. She might be a size sixteen, maybe a tinge bigger if the outfit ran small, but her tailor was a genius.

A soft cashmere suit in claret red draped lightly over her body. The deep U of a satin camisole exposed creamy cleavage. Her long hair was usually in a French twist or up in a chignon, but not tonight. She wanted a soft image. Loose almost-black curls brushed her shoulders.

As usual, spike heels added to her already striking five foot eleven inch height. Sheer black stockings flattered her legs. She chose a lacy garter belt instead of panty hose. Just in case.

A lightweight short mink jacket and her signature three-carat diamond stud earrings completed the look.

At exactly seven, the uniformed chauffeur driving a Mercedes limo was in the driveway. She was outside before he texted.

The driver smiled politely and helped her into the back seat. *Wow. This one's gorgeous. Definitely class all the way. Lucky guy.*

"Any special music you'd prefer, Ma'am?"

"Yes. A classical station please. Soft. I want to relax."

"The gentleman sent champagne. Shall I pour you a glass?

"What kind?"

"Bollinger, Ma'am"

"Sure, I'll have a glass. You can leave the bottle handy."

Ben never does things on the cheap, anyway.

The chauffeur drove carefully and sneaked peeks in the rear view mirror. She leaned against the leather headrest, her suit jacket opened. The light mink was draped across her shoulders. She didn't initiate conversation.

Glad the lady decided to get comfy. Wow. That neckline shows her off nice. I'll be sorry to see this ride end.

CHAPTER 28
THE FIGHT

"Gino, it's hard to believe Frankie's old enough to be your partner. I used to carry him around on my shoulders when you first opened the place."

The handsome, broad shouldered young man had just refreshed Ben's Scotch and his father's Bourbon.

"You two better take it slow, Pop. Probably can't hold the booze the way you used to." His smile was wide as he ducked Gino's playful cuff.

"That was over twenty-five years ago, old friend. He turned out OK. Loved the food business since he could walk. Wanted to skip college to come work here. His Mama, god rest her soul, and I told him no way. Had to get an education. Ended up graduating with honors in business."

"Went to Bentley, didn't he?"

"Yeah. Glad Maria lived to see that."

"How long has it been?"

"Twelve years and I still miss her."

"No lady in your life?"

"A couple nice women here and there, but nothing serious. I'd like to find someone. Lousy to be alone. You?"

"Long story Gino. Hope there's a happy ending."

Frankie poked his head into Gino's office. "Limo's close. Driver called to say he's ten minutes out."

Ben left his Scotch. "I'd better be at the door. Want to make this as easy as I can."

"This lady I must meet. I'm coming with you."

Gino's patrons were used to the occasional celebrity, but Ollie had her charisma meter set on high. There was a tiny lull in the conversation when she made her entrance.

Frankie was star-struck behind the host's desk.

She hugged Ben. "I'm impressed. How did you ever get a table here on a Saturday night? Have you got an in with the management or something?"

"Matter of fact, I do. Ollie, meet Gino."

"I am honored, Madame." Gino bent from the waist as he lifted Ollie's hand to his lips. "Welcome."

His son's expression remained enthralled. "Please, may I introduce my business partner, who is also my son, Franco."

Ollie was enjoying the younger man's reaction to her. "How nice to meet you both." Her smile deepened for Frankie's benefit.

Ben sensed she had finished holding court. He took her mink jacket, admired her cleavage in spite of himself, and followed Gino to their dining room.

There was a bottle of champagne chilling. "Courtesy of Franco and me," Gino told them.

"Oh my goodness, Ben. This is pretty special. You're forgiven for not coming to get me."

There was a soft knock on the door. Frankie came in carrying Ben's untouched Scotch.

"Dad said you'd probably prefer this to champagne. Ma'am, would you prefer something else to drink as well?"

"No, I'm more of a champagne lady. But you're sweet to offer." She stood very straight with her jacket opened to let Frankie admire her.

He colored just a bit and left quickly. Ben knew she was amusing herself. He was annoyed but relieved at the same time. She seemed to be in a half-decent mood.

As soon as they were sitting and alone, she started. "I think we need to talk. You texted me that you felt that way too."

"Hey, food first. By the way, you are gorgeous tonight." *But you know that very well, don't you, Ollie? And the games don't stop. You deliberately made that kid crazy about you in two minutes.*

"Thank you." *You didn't kiss me when I came in though, and you haven't yet. Not sure I like this vibe.*

A waiter brought menus and an assortment of appetizers, again, courtesy of the management.

Ollie wanted to start with a Caesar Salad. "No anchovies, please. I hate the ugly little things. I'll have the Salmon a la Gino's for the main course. I've heard so much about it."

Ben gave her order and asked the waiter for a Caprese salad. "Would you have Gino choose a simple shrimp dish for me? No pasta please."

"Absolutely Mr. Whitcomb. I'll be back shortly." He left quietly, closing the silk-draped French doors behind him.

"Good thing I caught your text this morning, Ollie. Would've been something if I was in New York to keep our late lunch date and you were here. Phone company had a glitch yesterday and some texts and emails got lost."

Getting pretty good at deception, aren't you, Mate? Better than dealing with her in a tantrum though.

"Well, you said you had to be back in Boston tonight, and my schedule changed a little. I can stay for a few days. Thought I'd make it easy for you." *Wonder what took up most of the day you'd planned to fly down to be with me?*

"Nice of you. Turns out, I was able to spend the afternoon on some of the work I was going to do tonight after I got back. Gave me a chance to take you here. Do you like it?"

"Of course I do! It's one of the best hidden gems for food in Boston. You getting VIP treatment makes it extra special."

I'm starting to think there are some things I don't know about you, Ben. Like how come you haven't touched me yet.

"Let me refill that champagne."

"No thanks. I had a glass or two in the limo. You were thoughtful to send it…being so angry about me calling the boys and all."

The waiter arrived with the salads. Frankie was along to be sure everything was perfect.

"Franco, would you mind keeping Ms. Poulas company for a few minutes? Have a glass of that nice champagne you sent us."

"No champagne, Ben, I'm working. However, nothing would give me more pleasure than to keep…"

"Forget the Ms. Poulas. I'm Ollie to you, Franco." She leaned over to pat Ben's vacated chair. Frankie tried not to look at her magnificent breasts.

Ben found Gino. "Look, I can't hold the conversation off much longer. I know she'll be livid, and will probably make a dramatic exit. Could Frankie make sure she has a limo home?"

"I don't want to pry, here, but are you two seeing each other? Because if not, my son would give a month's salary to take her home himself."

"Short version, we were, ah, involved for a while, up to a couple of years ago. Strictly friends since. She was fine with that until very recently. Seems she's looking for more at this point. Feeling's not mutual. Nice lady, but we didn't work out before and there's no chance now."

"Fine. I'll tell Frankie. Mamma mia, aren't you a little old for this?" Gino looked a lot more amused than concerned.

Ollie was giving Frankie one of her warmest smiles when Ben returned. The young man looked as if he had won the lottery.

"Thanks, Franco."

"The pleasure was all mine." He left quickly.

Hell, he's a lot closer to her age than I am. Maybe they'll hit it off.

After eating the salads, Ollie didn't want to wait any longer. She avoided his eyes first, then faced him contritely.

"Ben, I need to say this. I'm sorry Ryan and Pete were concerned after I called. All I said was you seemed a bit distracted. Asked if everything was OK. Nothing more."

His voice was just above a whisper. He looked straight at her with a steady gaze. "I think you wanted to find out if they knew why I wouldn't stay over after the game. Your ego was a bit bruised and you were annoyed. How right am I?"

She leaned toward him. "Well, you were damn close, Ben. We both know that. Then you turned off as if something hit you over the head. We were good together. Why not enjoy it?"

He leaned back in his chair. "We haven't been lovers for nearly a couple of years, Ollie. You're the one who said you wanted to explore other options."

The waiter knocked to bring the entrees and wine. They were quiet as he served and poured.

"Anything else, Sir?"

"No thanks. We'll be fine for a while."

She touched his arm. "That was a long time ago. It's out of my system. I'm ready to come back now, Ben."

He sat there, unsmiling and silent, without moving toward her.

"Your look says it all. You don't want me anymore." Her eyes moistened. "You let me make an ass out of myself tonight. Why didn't you do this over the phone? Is that why you wouldn't come to the condo? You thought I'd behave better in public."

The chair tipped as she bolted up. Her crystal glass shattered when it hit the wall. "You're a real bastard," she shouted.

She snatched her mink jacket from the seat next to her. "I'm going back to New York Monday afternoon. Don't come by for your stuff until then. I'm having the locks changed Tuesday."

"Ollie ..."

"Shut up Ben. I don't want to be your friend anymore." She flung the doors open, saying "Go screw yourself," loudly enough for most of the restaurant to hear. Then she marched toward the reception desk without tears but not trying to hide her fury.

Gino was standing by the bar when Ben came out of the dining room. "Wow. She's a little upset! Did she even touch her dinner?"

"Nope. Neither did I. Join me?"

"Why not? At least Frankie will be happy."

CHAPTER 29
ON THE ROAD

Angie turned on the morning news. "This will be the nicest early October day we could hope for. Temperature in the Boston area should be from 55 to 60, a bit lower in Western Mass. Not a cloud anywhere. It's perfect to get out and enjoy your Sunday folks!"

She was glad to see the weather for their leaf-peeping and sightseeing date was cooperating, although her stomach was queasy. *I've got butterflies. We had such a wonderful time Friday. Conversation was easy. I loved being with him. We had the movie to talk about though. Will we run out of things to say? Eventually we'll have to talk about what's going on in our lives now. Will we hate each other by the end of the day?*

What the hell was I thinking, plotting to seduce him? We're not planning to be gone overnight. Even if we did stay, it wouldn't necessarily mean we'd sleep together. She decided to stop overthinking and go downstairs for coffee. Drinking a cup always calmed her down.

A small tote she was taking had a change of undies, makeup, perfume, and a few toiletries. Those things took up very little room. *It's always good to be prepared for the unexpected.* She brought food, too.

When she and Dan were on a day trip, he always liked to have something to munch on, rather than stopping on the road for food he might not enjoy. He was fussy. No energy bars and crackers for him. He wanted good cheese, fruit, gourmet chocolate, nuts, and a bottle of nice wine in case they decided to picnic.

She decided to bring similar snacks for today. *He probably won't expect anything like this. It'll be fun to surprise him.*

Dan. They had a good life until he reached mandatory retirement age at 65. He repeatedly told her he was just as good as ever and shouldn't have to quit. Extreme skiing was the way he proved to himself he was still young. Then, he was gone. She stopped those thoughts. *No point in rehashing the past.*

Ben was due at nine. He was early the last time and now it was quarter to eight. She took the coffee upstairs.

I'm going to have fun today, and let things play out. No reason to be nervous. I haven't burned any bridges. My life doesn't have to change. Angie knew she was trying to reassure herself.

By eight-fifteen, she was showered, finished applying light makeup and had floated through a cloud of Chanel spray.

Fifteen minutes later, she was dressed. The copper-brown cord pants and creamy soft textured blouse looked good together. A forest green vest finished the outfit. Comfortable brown suede flat booties would be good for whatever walking they'd do. She'd take her light leather jacket in case the weather turned chilly. The satin and lace undies she wore made her feel sexy.

Fresh coffee finished brewing just as the bell rang at about eight forty-five.

He's early again. Good to plan for that little habit. "Why? You expecting this to be a regular thing?" she asked aloud. "Oh shut up!" she answered herself.

Angie opened the door with a smile. "Good morning, Ben. What a gorgeous day!" She stood on tiptoe to give him a quick kiss on the cheek.

He hugged her lightly. *She smells wonderful...like vanilla and spice. She's naturally pretty too. Doesn't need lots of makeup. What a lovely face to see in the morning.*

"And you're gorgeous too, Angela. I'm looking forward to having you for a whole day."

"You said we'd have brunch on the way, but I had toast and coffee earlier. Would you like anything before we start? Or should I just take a thermos for the trip?"

"A thermos would be just the thing. I grabbed a bite earlier as well."

"Great." She filled it and picked up the tote and her jacket. "May I toss these in the back seat? I've put a few things in we might use during the day. We'll keep the coffee in front if that's OK."

Ben took her jacket and the bag. "My goodness, this little thing weighs a ton. What've you got in there?"

"No peeking! Just a surprise or two."

He laughed, set the bag on the floor of the Land Rover and folded her jacket on the back seat. They were on the road by nine.

"Music?" he asked.

"That would be nice. You choose."

He put on a CD with Dvorak's *New World Symphony*.

"That's one of my favorites! It kind of goes with a beautiful sunny day."

He smiled, happy she liked his choice.

"Angela, as I recall, you preferred Broadway Musicals to light classical."

"Well, I enjoy both now, even symphony. My musical horizons have broadened over the years. Still don't like most opera."

I want to hold her hand. She seems to be enjoying herself so much. Maybe I was a damn fool to make such a big deal about her setting the pace.

The ride along the Mass Turnpike went fast. They listened to music, admired the colorful foliage, and chatted about how they both liked living close to the ocean. About two miles after taking the Lenox exit, Ben turned into the driveway of a picturesque gray-shingled inn.

"This is the place we're having brunch. Hope you'll like it."

Baskets of red and yellow chrysanthemums sat on low stone steps leading to the colonial door. An antique lantern in the circular reception room sparkled. Several rooms were visible through tall French doors.

Inside, a host greeted them. "Good morning, Mr. Whitcomb. Delighted to have you join us again." He nodded at Angie. "Hello Ma'am." He told Ben, "We have a table available for you in either room."

"Angela, would you prefer the small dining room or the patio? They have it heated. Either should be comfortable."

She looked around at the pretty surroundings. "Normally, I prefer outside, but that small room looks like an English library. Can we sit in there?"

"Of course we can."

The host settled them at a corner table, near large windows. "This gives you a nice view of the estate." He handed them menus. "May I bring you something to start? Champagne, a Mimosa or a Bloody Mary?" They both ordered Mimosas. Neither could hold back smiles.

She looked around, taking everything in. "I love this atmosphere. The paneled walls, framed hunting dog prints, and the antique-looking arm chairs are all perfect!"

"It reminds me of the library in my step-father's London home," he remarked.

She took a sip of her drink. "Do you go back there often?"

"Several times a year. Not as often as when Mum was alive. The people who handle family business over there are good."

What family business? And how often is several times a year? For that matter, where do you live most of the year? I noticed Florida plates on your car and the address on your business card.

Ben saw a questioning look flit across her face, but she picked up the menu without making a comment.

He hadn't touched his drink yet. There were some things to be said.

"Well, my lovely lady, anything strike your fancy?"

"Everything looks delicious. I'd be happy with a two-egg omelet, well done, avocado and bacon mixed in the eggs. Tomato slices instead of potatoes, please. And I think, since today is special, I'll have some cranberry-walnut rolls with sweet butter."

"Excellent. I'll have the same only with three eggs. Let me hail the server. OK if I give both orders?"

She looked at him with laughter in her eyes. "I'm interested in why you asked."

The corners of his mouth turned down a bit in embarrassment. "Sometimes, I forget and do ridiculously old-fashioned things that used to be considered good manners. However, I'd never want you to think I was presuming you weren't capable of speaking for yourself, Angela."

"I love you for that!" *Oh my god! What did I just say?* She felt that telltale blush creeping up. "Yes. Please do order for me."

He suppressed a laugh. She drank a large gulp of Mimosa.

"Angela." He said softly, "I enjoy being with you more than you can imagine. If you feel the same way, there are a few things I need to tell you."

She sat straight and her eyes widened. He could sense anxiety, and reached for her hand. Before she drew back from his touch, he felt it was ice cold. She looked away for a minute, then took a deep breath and met his warm gaze.

"Now that you mention it, Ben, yes. I do feel the same way. I'm happier with you than I've felt in a very long time. And that scares me."

"Don't let it. We feel the same way."

"Yes. But now I know enough to be careful not to chase a dream that has no chance of coming true."

"Does that mean you've even considered that something might be there for us?"

"Maybe." She looked down and shifted a bit in her chair.

His smiling face turned serious. He took a sip of his own drink. "Have you changed your mind since the other night when you said I might have a tiny chance with you?"

"No, not really." She faced him again and leaned forward. "This whole thing, meeting you again out of the blue, feeling as if we're old friends, well, it's overwhelming. If I do give it, or us, or whatever, a chance, you'll have to be very honest with me."

"Ask me anything. Will you trust my answers?"

She put her hand on the table between them, palm up. "Why wouldn't I? You've never lied to me that I can remember." He squeezed her hand and let go.

Only once, my love, when I told you we couldn't make a life together.

She looked into his eyes. "There's nothing that can change the past, so we can discuss all of that later if we need to." Sitting back in her chair, her expression was serious and her voice was low but strong. "Here's what I have to know now. Are you free, legally and emotionally, to take whatever might develop between us the whole distance? However it turns out?"

He took his time responding, a little astonished at her direct approach.

She's courageous and honest. It wasn't easy for her to be so blunt. I asked for it though. At least the answer is easy.

"Wow. You don't sugar-coat questions, do you?"

"Not the time to play games, is it?" At least she was smiling.

"Well, Madame Inquisitor, let me be just as direct. I am free, in every way. There are no wives, separated partners, legal entanglements, or warrants for my arrest. There are two sons that I love very much. However, they should present no problem in the pursuit of 'whatever might develop between us,' as you put it."

He reached for his Mimosa and finished half of it in one gulp.

Angie relaxed in her chair with a sweet smile. "OK then, Ben. Let's see what happens."

At that moment, breakfast arrived.

As they ate, he told her, "You can be a formidable woman, Angela. I am seldom intimidated."

"It's good for you once or twice in a lifetime, Ben."

He laughed softly. "If you say so, my love."

CHAPTER 30

IN THE BERKSHIRES

They lingered over coffee, smiling, chatting about the lovely inn, and thinking how nice it was to be together.

"The grounds have all kinds of pretty paths to wander. Shall we try to work off a little breakfast?"

"That's a great idea. Let me stop into the ladies' room and we'll go."

Probably should have mentioned Ollie during that bit where she asked if I were absolutely free. I'll have to bring it up. How could I have been so damn stupid to think that woman only wanted me for a condo sitter? I should have bailed out last weekend when she came on to me. Hope Angela has a complication or two as well. Maybe that Charlie chap.

She came toward him, her brown eyes smiling and short thick red curls framing her sculptured face. *Oh my god. She's even more attractive to me now than she was when we were young. The laugh lines make her look interesting as well as lovely.*

They headed onto a wooded path, colorful with red, orange, gold and green fall foliage. Content to hold hands and enjoy the colors, they were comfortably silent.

"Let's take a quick selfie," Angie suggested. "The trees will make a pretty background. We can set the phone on that stone wall and prop it up with something."

"Will this be the first record of us together?" he asked.

She let go of his hand and walked toward the wall, her back to him. "Not really. I have one or two others."

He caught up quickly and turned her to face him. "Angela! You honestly saved some?"

"Just two of my favorites. I haven't looked at them in decades. They're imprinted on my brain." She lowered her head to avoid his gaze.

He gently raised her chin. "Was one of them when we walked through the Commonwealth Ave. Mall with the cherry blossoms in full bloom? You wore that yellow blouse with a matching print skirt. It was warm for spring. We stopped for coffee at the sidewalk café on Newbury Street after. That photo was beautiful, because of both you and the setting."

She nodded and her eyes misted. *There's not a lot he's forgotten either.*

With his hand still under her chin, he bent, kissed her gently and hugged her. She stood, arms at her sides, saying nothing, snuggled into his chest.

After a moment, he let her go. "Let me see if I can get the phone propped and the settings done. Unless, of course, you think your mechanical abilities are better than mine?"

Her laughter lightened the mood. They did a few poses, chuckling at the theatrics.

"We'll never get to Stockbridge and the museums if we keep wandering through the estate," he remarked.

"It's fine," she answered. "I can't remember the last time I got to enjoy the fall colors. It's my favorite time of year."

"We must be a mile in by now. At my advanced age, I could use a rest. Shall we sit on that little bench for a few minutes?"

"Sure. I know old folks can lack stamina," she responded with mock concern. *You may not be young, but you are gorgeous.*

Angie looked appreciatively at his trim athletic body, with well-toned muscles evident in the tailored pants and sweater. Silver gray hair sparkled in the early afternoon sun. Jogging, sailing, and playing tennis left a light tan on his expressive face. His eyes smiled as they focused on her.

He hooked her waist with a long arm and pulled her onto his lap. "You have turned into a little smart-ass, haven't you? I should make you pay for that crack. However, because I am a proper British gentleman, I shall let it pass." He deposited her next to him on the bench. "Besides, I need your advice."

"Yes?"

"You remember I was condo sitting in Plover Cove for an old friend who's on a business trip?"

"Uh-huh."

"Well, there were some complications. I left without much notice, then got thrown out anyway, and I'm at the Washington Hotel in Salem for a while."

"Complications. Care to say more?" Angie moved a little further away from him.

He let her.

"You might say I've been a total idiot and very naïve. My friend is the lady I was involved with a couple of years ago. She's probably an ex-friend now anyway. We cleared the air last night."

Last night! Wonder what happened? I was right about taking things slow. Very slow.

Ben saw her body tense as she stood to face him.

"Ben, this is probably none of my business. But now that you're telling me, how come it didn't come up when we were talking about entanglements a while ago?" Her voice was edgy.

"Because that's not what this is. Ollie usually wants what she can't have. We had agreed at the start of this sitting thing that she wouldn't return to the condo until the day I was due to leave. That's in about three weeks. She broke the promise. End of story."

Angie frowned and looked away. She turned abruptly and started down the path fast.

"Angela, for heaven's sake. I want to tell you everything about this."

"Don't bother, Ben. No need for explanations." She sounded as if she were choking back an angry response.

"Well, you're not absolutely saintly, now, are you? Good thing I'm seeing this bit of bad temper. Please. Give me the courtesy of letting me explain."

She whirled around, hurt and anger in her eyes. "You said we could take little breaks from each other today if we needed them. Maybe this would be a good time."

He touched her shoulder lightly. She turned away again, but stayed still, listening.

"I saw the lights on in the condo after I left you Friday night. Thought someone had broken in, actually. Sneaked around like a thief, saw her things in the living room. I grabbed my computer before she heard me, and ran like hell. Didn't bother with clothes or anything else. Figured she'd probably throw my stuff on the beach after I straightened things out...which I did last night."

"Well, you look well-dressed." She turned to look at him with an unreadable face.

"The hotel concierge set me up to get a few things."

"Oh, my." The anger had disappeared and her laughter was genuine. "Just thinking about you being terrified enough to run away is too funny. Did it all work out when you had a chance to talk?"

"If you don't count the shattered glass and a loud declaration to an entire restaurant that I am the world's worst bastard, I suppose you could say it wasn't a disaster."

"Can you get the rest of your stuff?"

"Don't know, don't care. Only thing that matters is that we're OK. Even if you are huffy and high-handed."

She thought about her own date with Charlie the night before. She hadn't exactly broken anything off.

I didn't tell him about how close I am to Charlie, either. We both have things going on. If it's to work out, it will.

"Guess we don't have time for a break from each other. If you don't have any other little news updates, let's both try to behave and explore this beautiful area."

They wandered back toward the inn, saying little, but holding hands.

That could have gone a lot worse. She is a wise woman. Knows when to let things lie.

Bet he hasn't heard the last of that woman.

As they drove to town, a huge stone mansion with smaller buildings sat on acres of manicured grounds off the road.

"Ben, is that the *Wellington?* I've heard so much about it. The spa is supposed to be incredible."

"I've heard that as well. Reviews say the whole resort has perfect service, not stuffy, and something for everyone."

"It's always booked solid, I think," she remarked.

He made a mental note to himself.

They arrived in Stockbridge with enough time to visit the museum and sightsee before it got dark. Ben made a quick call while Angie visited the gift shop.

"I'll do my very best, Mr. Whitcomb," the credit card VIP concierge told him. "You'll have a text within fifteen minutes."

"Thanks, Eddie. I know it's an almost impossible request."

Eddie worked for one of the most prestigious credit card companies in the world. Ben Whitcomb was an excellent customer and a nice person too. He wanted to pay for a suite at the *Wellington* with two separate bedrooms whether he used it or not. Eddie knew lots of people. He'd make that happen.

Ben found Angela buying some note cards. When she finished, she looked concerned.

"It's getting dark. We've been on the go all day. I'm not the best on highways at night, but why don't you let me drive for a while going home? It'll give you a chance to relax."

"That's a lovely gesture, but I'm quite used to long drives. I've made it from Florida to Cambridge in two days. I have a place in Naples."

Ahh. That explains the plates. He must spend most of the year there.

"Well, the offer's open. I'm having such a wonderful time it's too bad we can't stay longer. But, no sense trying to sightsee in the dark."

They walked toward the parking lot.

He took the opportunity immediately. "Do you have important work obligations tomorrow?"

"No. Thought it would be a good idea to take the day off in case we got back late."

He stopped and turned to face her. "Then should we consider staying over and playing hooky tomorrow? We could plan to start back around three or so. I know a nice place for dinner near route two. That would let us avoid rush hour. We'd be home by eight."

Angie looked uncertain.

"It's tourist time, Ben. Could we find a decent place?"

I'm going to leave it to him to sort out sleep accommodations. Let's see if he asks about separate rooms.

"Maybe. If not, well, that's that."

Eddie had texted him that there was a suite with a separate bedroom and a very comfortable sleep sofa. Ben took it for the night with a late checkout in the morning.

Let's see how she reacts.

"Isn't this the *Wellington?*" she asked when they took a right onto the long driveway.

"Well, I thought we could give it a try since we've both heard such good things."

"Ben, you have to let me split the bill if they do have something." *Can't let him pay for this place. It probably starts at five hundred a night for a room.*

"No worries. It's on the company."

"What company?"

He turned to her, saying innocently, "Mine. I own a couple."

Her mouth dropped open just a bit.

"Explanations later. We can just add it to the list of things to talk about sometime. C'mon!"

He parked, opened her door, and grabbed her tote from the back along with a small one of his own that she hadn't noticed. She took her jacket.

"You always travel with an overnight kit, Ben?"

"Old habit from driving so much. Always keep a few things in the car in case of emergencies." *Except for the other night. Never thought I'd need it.*

She could have sworn she saw him smile in the twilight.

The *Wellington* reception area was more like a country house library than the usual lobby. A small space adjacent to the main room had someone sitting at a large cherry table.

"Let me see what I can do," Ben said, "I'll be just a minute."

She stood looking at an impressive oil painting when he returned.

"They have something. Do you want to see if it's OK before we register?"

She looked at his hopeful face and suddenly had no doubt what she wanted.

"No. If it sounds good to you, I trust your judgment."

His hazel eyes crinkled in a smile.

CHAPTER 31

BERKSHIRE MUSIC

When Ben opened the door to their suite, Angie was stunned.

"This is like something out of a decorator's dream house!"

A huge white-mantled fireplace warmed the large square room. At six, it was late enough to be dusk. A wall of windows framed the full moon hovering over banks of trees. Soft lighting complemented the long cream-colored sofa in front of the fireplace. Arm chairs, covered in cream and maroon striped damask material, sat by the window. A three-quarter bath was tucked next to the closet in the foyer.

"The manager said there's a separate bedroom behind the French doors."

She opened them to see another large room decorated in soft hues of white, cream, and light green. The king-sized bed fit easily, along with mahogany side tables and a large chest of drawers. A green Aubusson rug covered most of the gleaming hardwood floors.

"How beautiful! These are my favorite colors!"

He smiled, happy with her reaction. *Good. She likes everything so far. Better clear up the sleeping arrangements right away. Don't want her to be upset.*

Unless she's changed her mind about…? Uh-uh Mate. All you can do is hope. She'll let you know. Or not.

"The large room is yours, of course. The sofa opens to a king-sized bed, large enough to accommodate me. So everything is quite proper as well."

"Thank you. I do appreciate that consideration," Angie told him.

The marble master bath with a double glass shower and a jetted tub was down a short, closet-lined hall from the bedroom. Multiple toiletries, including shaving equipment, toothbrushes and toothpaste sat on the mirrored dressing table. She noticed the soaps, lotions, and hair products were all a top French brand.

"Oh, my goodness, Ben. I'm not sure I've ever stayed anywhere this luxurious."

"Both the tavern and the dining room are good from what I've been told. They're open until ten-thirty. Shall we raid the minibar, have a drink here first, then go down and decide where we want to eat? Or are you starving now?"

She smiled at him. *Damn straight, I'm starving. Not for food though.*

"A drink sounds lovely, but we may be able to do better than the minibar selections. Hang on a sec."

She pulled a bottle of Balvenie Portwood Single Malt Scotch, 21 years old, out of her tote.

"Angela! This is for connoisseurs. How did you choose it?"

It is a splurge, but he's fed me several times. That orchid was probably more expensive than the Scotch. Considering what this suite must be costing, I'm glad I got it for him.

"Well, I *like* good Scotch, but I usually drink white wine when I'm out. It's not as strong, and I can make it last a long time."

Ben was impressed. The bottle was extremely expensive. He was delighted by her thoughtfulness, and gave her a light hug and kiss.

"Will you have some if I open it now?" He asked.

"Love to."

There were crystal glasses on the wet bar in the corner of the room.

"Any special way you like it?"

"Yes, please. Add just a splash of water. That's how they did it in Scotland."

She reached back into the tote for an insulated bag. The large block of cheese was still chilled and she had gourmet crackers as well.

"Here are some snacks we didn't use in our travels today. Let's have them now."

"What else do you have in that magic bag, Angela?" Ben smiled in appreciation.

"My secret, Sir. I pull things out as needed."

She brought the tote into the bedroom and put it on top of the chest of drawers. Angie wanted it to be handy if things went as she hoped.

Ben prepared the drinks. The room was warm. She took off her vest. The soft blouse, although not transparent, draped to reveal her curves.

"Ben, aren't you very warm in that sweater? Or is it just me?"

"Actually, I am." He got up, took it off, and hung it in the closet. Angie admired his tall, lean body.

Now, now, no need to rush this, girl. Remember what he used to like.

She put the drinks and cheese on the coffee table while Ben explored what was in the CD cabinet. "What kind of music would you like? We have classical, popular, Beatles, jazz, rock, folk and Bennett and Sinatra."

"Oh, how about Frank? His music fits the setting." *It fits my purpose, too.*

Finally, they were sitting next to each other on the comfortable sofa, not yet touching.

"Here's to wonderful road trips," Angie toasted.

"And to beautiful traveling companions," Ben added.

They sipped the Scotch and quietly enjoyed the fire for a few minutes. Sinatra crooned about September and life passing. She turned to him with a warm smile and asked, "Do you still dance, Ben?"

"On special occasions, Angela."

I remember she used to love slow dancing to Sinatra. Sometimes more than dancing happened when we did that. I can only hope.

"Would you consider this a special occasion?" She mimicked his formality.

"I'd say so, yes."

She stood and took his hand. His eyes had a smoky look when he got up. They swayed to the music for a while, with her head resting just below his shoulder and her arms wrapped around his neck.

In a soft sexy voice, she murmured. "Ben, I need to ask you something."

"Mmmm?" He was lost in her scent, and the feel of her in his arms. He wasn't sure how much longer he could hold himself back.

"Would you be upset if we didn't use the sofa and the bedroom?"

Ben pulled back to look at her. "Angela, are you saying you don't want to stay here after all? Do you want to go home?"

He sounded incredulous, but not angry.

"Oh, no! Please don't misunderstand. It was wonderful of you to be so considerate about getting sleeping arrangements you thought would put me at ease. But Ben, I don't want us to be in separate beds."

Oh god, don't you get it? You wanted me to make the next move. That's what I'm doing, damn it. Help me out here!

She reached up, pulled his head down and gave him a long, smoldering kiss. Their tongues explored, and their bodies molded together. She could feel his excitement.

"Angela." He held her body slightly away from him, looking into her passionate eyes. "There is nothing I want more than for us to make love to each other. Are you sure that's what you want too? "

"Yes, Ben. Oh yes, I do."

He returned her kiss with a slow and burning one of his own, then pulled the blouse out of her waistband and touched her silky skin with gentle fingers. She slipped her hands under his shirt, caressing his back and shoulders. Sinatra's music worked its magic as they held each other, swaying and kissing. Both were delighted to enjoy a slow and sensuous journey to their destination.

She unbuttoned his shirt, nuzzling his chest and making little mewls of pleasure as she took it off. He had all he could do not to take her then, but he was determined to pace himself for her pleasure.

Her blouse was easy to unbutton, revealing the beautiful, lacy, peach bra covering her in a filmy layer. He could see her excitement, as he teased the tops of her breasts with his tongue. She gasped, and ran her hands along his back, pulling him closer.

They kissed, nibbled, and explored each other as Sinatra sang. Finally, she took his hand and led him to the bedroom.

"Undress me, Ben?"

He kissed her deeply, then slipped off her slacks and his own. They stood facing each other, their excitement rising. The lovely bra held her breasts firm and high. Soft peach lace bikini panties invited him to explore.

She admired him standing bare chested, in blue tight fitting boxer-briefs that covered him from waist to mid-thigh. She wanted to kiss his belly. His excitement was obvious, but he was taking his time.

"Angela, I'm at a disadvantage." He whispered as he kissed the cleft between her breasts. "You have more clothes on than I have." He looked at her hungrily.

Her voice was seductive. "Well, can you fix that?"

Ben kissed her again, slowly, exploring her back from shoulders to where it joined her legs. His hands came back up, massaging her. He unhooked her bra and caressed her breasts slowly as he removed it. She stood only in her lacy bikini panties, her eyes nearly black with desire.

"You are beautiful, Angela." His voice was thick and his excitement was impossible to hide.

She pulled him into a hug that melded their bodies together. He kissed her hungrily and lifted her onto the high bed.

CHAPTER 32
BERKSHIRE ENCORE

Angie cuddled in Ben's arms, eyes closed, but awake. Her back muscles rippled in response to his gentle caresses.

He whispered into her hair. "You like being petted, do you?"

She pulled her head back from his shoulder. "Oh yes. And I liked everything else we did too, from slow start to crescendo finish."

He pulled her closer. "Well, you said you were out of practice. Thought we could start slowly and see how it went."

"And do you think it went well?" She teased.

"Ah, yes my love. So very well."

"Mmmm. Me too. What time is it?"

"Early, about eight-thirty."

"In the morning?" Angie looked puzzled. "It's dark out."

"No. Remember, you started to seduce me soon after we got here. We took a bit of a nap after we made love."

They both heard a soft growling noise in the quiet room.

"Angela! Is that your tummy?" He rubbed her abdomen and slithered down to listen. Then he laughed. "You're hungry! I remember cooking you pancakes at two in the morning back in the day."

"And do you remember what usually happened? After I was fed? To show my appreciation for your cooking?"

He kissed her breast. "Let's eat. If we get room service, there's no need to dress."

"Yes, and then we'll be distracted and the food will get cold."

"And how is that bad, my love?"

"You're indecent!" she squirmed out of his reach, and sat up, forgetting the soft light was on and she was naked. "Besides, don't you want to see this place after your company paid a fortune for the suite?"

"My dear," he groaned, "all I want to see right now is more of you."

She pulled the sheet around her. "Ben, I'm starved."

He tried to look disappointed, but his eyes sparkled. "You win. Let's shower."

"Separately, this time. So we actually do go for dinner… or at least a snack."

He didn't let that pass. "This time? Does that mean that I may have you for a companion in a future shower?"

She loved seeing him enjoy her playfulness. "Maybe. Feed me well, and perhaps we get to make love again. Just to make sure we did it perfectly the first time."

Although if that wasn't perfect, I don't know what is. And it wasn't just sex. We really wanted to please each other. Last time I felt like that was with him, but he's better now. The passion is still there, but he's added patience. He found places to kiss that I'd never imagine.

She blushed and shivered on the way to the bathroom. "Be out in a few minutes."

He enjoyed watching her move, without any effort to cover herself from his hungry eyes. *She wants to keep me hot. Some things haven't changed about her. Not lean and hard as back then, but she feels so good. She was shy at first, too. The payoff was worth every second I spent getting her there.*

"I'll be quicker, my love. Don't forget I have my own shower."

In just a few minutes, she came into the bedroom, this time in a black lace bra and matching bikinis. *He still loves lacy undies. Glad I packed a couple of extra sets.*

Ben had shut the door so she could dress in privacy.

He isn't missing a beat. Tomorrow we need to get back to reality. Tonight, well, tonight is the fantasy I dreamed of for years. I'm going to enjoy every second.

When Ben called for reservations, the operator assured him there'd be a table for two available in either the pub or the formal dining room.

"I think something light will be fine. Maybe a crab cake and a salad," she said.

"Whatever you crave, Angela. I'm sure they'll serve us anything we want in either place. Just a matter of which you like better."

That's the thing about getting a top suite. People are very accommodating. Whatever it costs, it's worth that and more. She's decided to let herself see what happens, at least for the weekend. I'll take it for now and be glad.

They found the pub more appealing than the dining room. Their table was secluded, overlooking a lighted rock garden with pots of greenery.

After he seated them, the host asked, "May we buy you both a drink, Mr. Whitcomb, to welcome you to the *Wellington* for your first stay?"

"Would you like something, Angela?"

"A glass of cabernet would be good." She smiled appreciatively at the host. "How nice of you to offer."

"And I'll have the same. Thank you," Ben told him.

"You're always pleasant to people, Angela. I love that about you."

"Oh, I can get in a snit every now and then when people are rude or hurtful."

"Yes. I saw a flash of that temper today. Good for you. Hated to be on the receiving end, but you can't let people walk all over you either." He leaned across the table. "Actually that tartness is attractive."

She whispered in his ear," Watch who you call a tart, Sir! Or maybe I'll need to be less accommodating."

This time, he blushed. "Angela, that's not what I meant and you know it!"

The waiter arrived with the drinks and a plate of assorted cheeses.

Smiling, she toasted in a soft voice. "Here's to a wonderful reprise, very soon."

"Let's hurry and eat," he responded.

They settled for hamburgers and onion soup. Angela's eyes gleamed at the thought of bread pudding on the dessert menu. "It's my all-time favorite, but too much of an extravagance."

When the waiter brought the bill, Ben said, "We'll have two bread puddings to go. Extra whipped cream." Angela chuckled.

"We'll be glad to send that to your suite, Mr. Whitcomb."

"No, thanks anyway. We'll take it with us."

She smiled. "No interruptions that way."

At her insistence, they took a quick look at the opulent spa, and visited the solarium on the way back to the room. He kissed her, saying, "The bread pudding is getting cold."

She answered mischievously, with a question. "Are you getting cold too?"

"No. I am definitely not."

"Then, shall we go and resume our activities?"

The maid had been busy. Bathroom linens were fresh, and the bed was changed and turned down. Their two nearly untouched glasses of exquisite Scotch sat on the coffee table with a plate of chocolate truffles. The lights were soft, and classical music played from the radio.

They looked at each other and at the same time, said, "Wow!"

"Ben, could we take just a quick look at the news? I'm a junkie when it comes to what's happening around the world. Would you mind? We can watch while we finish those drinks. The Scotch is too good to waste, and we're not driving."

"I do not believe this. Another habit we share. When did you develop an interest in hard news?"

"When I realized the world didn't revolve around me, I guess."

She disappeared into the master bath and returned barefoot, wrapped in an oversized terry robe. "Found this by the shower. There's another if you want it."

He reached for her. "Anything on under it?"

She dodged him. "If you're good, I may let you find out. First, Scotch and news."

They sat on the couch for a while. Ben sneaked the hand that was over her shoulder into the open edge of the robe. He nuzzled her. She sighed with pleasure, stood, and opened the robe.

He groaned. "You certainly know how to dress for success, my love. Little bits of black lace suit your coloring."

"Well, here's your choice. You can admire my outfit, or, if you prefer, take it off."

She snaked around him and into the bedroom. His clothes were off in seconds. It took much longer to remove hers, because he kissed and nipped every bit of what he uncovered.

They made love to each other for hours before falling into an exhausted, happy sleep.

At about four AM, Ben fed Angie some bread pudding. She showed her appreciation and they slept again, holding each other.

He awakened at eight-thirty in the morning and covered her with the light sheet and blanket. Then he put on coffee. She had told him she liked a cup the minute she got up.

Never, before I met her, or since I left, have I been so happy and content. She'll need time to trust me again. And I'll die before deliberately hurting her, no matter what.

He was sitting in the bedroom chair, drinking coffee. The aroma woke her, but she didn't stir.

I'm going to give us some time. Nobody else makes me feel like this. I'll be careful, but what if this is really a second chance? Angie ignored the inner voice telling her she was an idiot.

She opened her eyes. He was watching her intently. They greeted each other at the same time.

"Good morning, Love."

CHAPTER 33

HEADING HOME

"Well! That greeting deserves a kiss." He unfolded himself from the easy chair and walked barefoot toward the bed. The covers slipped from her shoulders as she sat up.

"Angela!" He hugged her." I planned a quick good morning greeting, but you are much too tempting."

She grabbed for the covers, but not before he managed to hold her closely and drop his lips to her warm breasts.

She held him there for a few seconds, kissing the top of his head.

"I'm beginning to think you're only after my body!"

"Well, lovely lady, not exclusively. But it certainly is part of your allure. After your intellect and good taste, of course."

"Coffee. Now. Would you mind pouring me a cup?" She wrapped herself in the sheet and grabbed the robe at the bottom of the bed.

"May I help you with that?"

"No, thank you. I need some privacy. Then, when I come out there, we'll discuss today's activities." She gave him a little mock glare. "Which will involve being fully dressed and upright."

"There you go again. Getting snippy and giving orders." He ducked away from the pillow she tossed.

When she joined him, wrapped in the white robe, coffee was on the table by the windows, giving Angie a panoramic view of sparkling foliage. Ben had put a little dish of bread pudding next to it.

He was sitting across the table, scanning the newspaper. "Well, since my advances aren't welcome, I guess I'll settle for watching you be happy." He looked over the edge of the paper with a cocked eyebrow.

"Ben, can we go to the Clark Art Museum? It has a magnificent collection of Impressionists."

"Of course. You might like a few antique stores and rare book places too."

She took her coffee to the end of the long window. "Isn't that view amazing?"

"Indeed it is, my love." He stood and gazed at her. "Are you enjoying this weekend?"

She turned, with a quizzical expression on her face. "Do you want the absolute truth?"

His face fell.

"Oh, Ben. I'm teasing!" She said, hugging his waist. "This weekend is one of the best I've ever had."

"And why is that Angela?" his tone was carefully neutral.

She laughed merrily, not moving away from him. "Well, let's see. Hard to say really. The scenery is spectacular. Food is wonderful. Both the inn where we had brunch and this estate are charming." By this time, she was leaning back and looking straight into his eyes.

"And you're a delightful conversationalist. Oh yes, one last thing." She said, kissing his neck. "You're passionate, gentle, considerate and a marvelous lover."

He hugged her tightly.

"Ben," she told him, her face against his shoulder, "I haven't felt this, well, desirable, for a lot of years. Even if I know it's a fantasy, I'll cherish this weekend forever."

"Fantasy? How do you mean?" He gently slipped out of her arms, poured fresh coffee for them both, and led her to sit on the couch, facing him.

"We've been back in each other's life for a week. We both have friends, obligations, things we're involved in. The worlds that we've each built over the years...with the people who've been such great supports."

He spoke softly. "Since we've enjoyed being together so much, I think we might be able to work each other into our worlds, don't you?"

She took his hand. "I'd love that. But, it might be tough to accept some of the old friends."

She means Charlie, I'm sure. It will be damn tough, but I'll need to deal with it. I'm not feeling that she's bothered by Ollie. Might be, if she knew about the six texts asking to talk since Saturday night.

"Well, let's enjoy the rest of today, my love." He stood and stretched. "How about I order some breakfast to be delivered in an hour or so? That will give us time to shower and dress."

"There's a plan. Omelet for me, please." She finished her coffee and headed for the master bedroom.

"May I come?" he asked. "You did sort of promise yesterday you'd let me join you for a shower."

"OK. But just to scrub my back. And maybe wash my hair if you want to."

"Absolutely." He tried to look innocent. "I'll wash every strand."

They swayed together a little under the gentle rain shower, getting lavender soap to foam. She shivered in response to his gentle full body massage.

"Ben! We're supposed to be washing. This is definitely not the way I wash."

"Just want to make sure not to miss an inch of you. You can do the same for me."

His knees almost gave way as she followed his lead. "Angela," he said, gasping, "You may be the reason I drown in here!"

After leisurely and meticulous attention to each other, they emerged from the shower flushed and satisfied.

"Well, we compromised." Ben couldn't stop grinning. "You said all our activity today would be dressed and upright. We stayed mostly upright."

"One of us did, anyway." She answered, blushing.

They were wrapped in huge warmed towels when the bell to the suite rang. Ben put on a robe. "Room service is very efficient, isn't it?" He managed a leer. "Are you sure you don't need my help to dry anywhere?"

"I'll do fine." She couldn't help smiling.

Angie decided to dress before she joined him for breakfast.

"You look very proper and pretty," he told her when she walked into the living room. "Who would know what a temptress you really are?"

"Only you, Sir." She shot him a come-hither look. "And I hope you keep it in mind."

By eleven, they were at the museum, looking at famous Impressionist paintings.

"Have you been to Monet's home in France, Ben? The gardens are exactly as he painted them."

"Yes, I have. There's a special light reflected in those scenes, don't you think?"

Standing shoulder to shoulder, they delighted in wandering through the exhibits. "Something else we both enjoy," she remarked.

She didn't see his pleased expression.

Wonder if Charlie ever takes her to museums? Wonder if they ever...? Whitcomb, you stupid sod, what difference? She said it's been years. Let it go. You were no saint with Ollie.

It was one o'clock before they knew it. "Are you hungry?" he asked her.

"Not really. A coffee would be good though."

It was warm enough to enjoy a leisurely cup on the terrace of an outdoor café. They compared their reactions to the different artists, not altogether surprised they seemed to enjoy the same ones. After excursions to a rare bookstore and then to a couple of antique shops, it was three-thirty.

He looked at his watch, took her hand and said, "If we're to get back around eight and you'll still have dinner with me at a lovely little place on the way, we need to get going, my love."

"OK." She turned to face him. "Thank you for this, Ben." He was touched to see her eyes mist.

"It's only the start."

"But it is just a start, you know." She took her hand from his. "There are no guarantees. You did what you had to do

back then, Ben. I respect that. But I remember the pain."
She dropped her eyes."

"Angela. I was a panicked, self-centered, spoiled fool.
Raising two boys and marrying just to be able to give them
stability will grow one up at warp speed."

"Let's just enjoy what we have for now," she responded,
"because it's wonderful."

They drove down Route 2 as the sun was setting. She was
thrilled with the *Watershed* restaurant, fascinated by tim-
bered ceilings and old construction. Ducks swam in the
lake and lanterns flickered in the twilight.

"The end of a perfect day," she said.

His eyes held mischief. "Not quite the end, is it?"

"Tomorrow's a work day. And I have observant neighbors. Besides, we agreed. After our morning, at least all the
rest of the day would be spent fully dressed!"

His low laugh and wicked grin made her blush.

Over steaks, "We used a lot of calories over the weekend,"
Ben justified their meal, they discussed the week ahead.

She listened as he told her about Pete and Ryan's business deal. "Because of it, I'm without a place to live." He
watched for her reaction to his next idea.

"Living in Cambridge wasn't as convenient as I thought.
Traffic is always vicious, and, as it turns out, I don't need a
formal Boston office." He took a sip of the smooth Merlot.
"I find the North Shore beautiful, close to the airport, and
full of interesting places. Thought I might try to rent a spot
in Rock Harbor or Plover Cove for a while."

Her eyes widened in surprise. "Don't you spend a lot of time in Florida during the year? And London now and then too?"

He reached for her hand. "Would you mind if I spent some time on your turf, Angela? I won't intrude on you, honestly. I've been asked to put together a book on business and part of the fall and early winter on the coast would be a good place to start it."

"Ben, of course I want you around. However…"

He took her hand and looked directly into her eyes. "You have a life. A very full one. We have no idea what's going to happen. You have friends who'll probably be suspicious of me, maybe jealous. OK. It might be messy here and there. However, I think we're worth a shot."

She was quiet for a moment. "I do too, but I'm still terrified of what might happen. I can't give up everything and everyone who's part of my life. That includes Charlie, Ben."

He looked away for a moment, but kept her hand in his.

She continued. "We've never been lovers. Not that he hasn't been hinting around, or that I haven't considered it. But he's also been a great friend and a big help with some legal issues. Besides, I like him."

"As I said. It might be messy here and there. I'll be nice to all your friends. Hell, you probably won't like all of mine either."

There was no one in the vicinity who didn't admire the attractive couple, obviously enthralled with each other.

Ben pulled the Land Rover into her driveway at eight-thirty. Without waiting, he got out, opened her door and grabbed her tote from the back seat.

"Let me get this for you. It certainly was a bag full of beautiful magic. Want me to bring in that Scotch for a nightcap?"

"You won't be staying that long." Her key opened the heavy door to soft lights.

He had her in his arms in seconds. "Just a goodnight kiss? Please?"

Her lips were on his. Their kiss was long and passionate.

"When will we see each other again, Angela?"

"I'm having dinner with Jake and Eileen tomorrow evening. They said to ask you to come, if you're free."

"I'm free, and I'd be delighted. Jake's a great old guy. I'd like to meet the lady who tamed him."

Angie smiled. "Until tomorrow, then."

They kissed again and held each other tightly.

"I'll call to say goodnight, my love."

She murmured, "Do. Please do."

As soon as he left, Angie went upstairs and changed into her flannel pants and oversized tee, then made hot cocoa. She checked phone messages and heard Charlie. "Guess you had a good time. Be careful, Gorgeous. People don't change all that much. I'm away this week on a cruise with Lily. Figured there was no reason not to go."

She added a small shot of brandy to the cocoa and took it up to bed.

Ben called at ten. "I miss you. Good night, Angela, my love."

"Me too. Sleep well, Love."

By ten-thirty, she regretted sending him back to his hotel. *I'm not sure what I'm feeling, but I need to be away from him to sort it out. At least for a night.*

CHAPTER 34
BACK TO REALITY

"Well, did you spend the weekend somewhere that specializes in rejuvenation, Angie? Your skin is glowing and you look happier than I've ever seen you." Her office manager's greeting was enthusiastic.

Helen's desk was at the front of the office where staff had their workspaces. Everybody in the area could hear her.

Anne Burke, RN, Vice-President of the company, came out of her office. "Tell me where you went, because I'm going to book a whole vacation week there if that's what happens in a long weekend." A short, pretty woman in her early forties, Anne was a single mom who had survived a nasty divorce. She came to work part-time when Angie first started the company ten years before, and got a Master's Degree in nursing while raising two girls.

Angie knew that Anne, with Helen's help, provided the same excellent service to their clients that she would herself. There was really no reason she had to work so much.

She smiled happily at both women who were friends as well as colleagues. "I had a nice time, ate well, and got more exercise than usual." *Wouldn't they enjoy details about that exercise?* "Now I need to catch up on what's been going on here. Let me get some coffee."

"I'll get it for you," Helen said. "Take a look at your email. When you've had a chance to catch up a little, can the three of us and Ken meet for a few minutes?"

"Problem?"

"Don't know yet. I'll round up Ken. A half-hour OK?" Anne asked.

"Sure." She was still distracted by everything that happened earlier in the morning.

Nan's text had arrived at six-thirty.

Didn't want 2 call n case u have guest. Call me later or i will haunt u all day. Tx for letting me kno u stayed ovrngt.

She answered the text only with the word 'Later'. Angie had emailed her friend saying not to expect her back until Monday morning. Jake's lights weren't on. That meant he was still at Eileen's or she was with him. Either way, he wouldn't be calling. *I'm not ready to talk to anyone yet.*

Her phone pinged a few minutes later at six forty-five. It was Ben.

Good morning, luv. If ur up, call me. Please? Here's cell n case u forgot.

She didn't wait to get coffee. He answered on the first ring. "I wanted to hear your voice. Any regrets, Angela?"

"None at all. I sent you home last night because I wanted a little time to think, not because I was upset about anything. We did abandon plans to take things slow."

"Yes, my love, we did. Now, since you made the first move this weekend, is it my turn next?"

"Ben!" she responded. "As I remember, you made enough moves in the shower yesterday to put you well ahead of your turn."

"You're blushing, aren't you, Angela?" He voice was full of mischief and glee.

"OK. I'm going to hang up on you now, before I get crazy." She shivered, remembering how he made her writhe in delight.

"No worries, I can be over in minutes to get you right. I'll make sure you get to work on time. Well almost on time. My appointment in Cambridge isn't until two."

"No. You stay away until tonight. We're due at Jake's at six."

"OK, lovely temptress. Shall I drop by an hour early?"

"It's a workday. I won't be home until quarter to six." She heard him chuckle, but just continued. "Good luck at the meeting. This is wonderful for Ryan and Pete. They must be thrilled."

"Thanks for remembering them Angela. It should be fine. I'm looking forward to tonight's dinner. Jake's probably done a full background check on me by now. He's a great friend to you. Bye my love."

"Wait, Ben."

"Yes? What did you forget?"

"I had a wonderful time this weekend. We did everything I enjoy doing…and some things I had forgotten how much I missed. Bye to you too, my love."

She clicked off quietly.

My love. He used to call me that before, too. It's probably a British version of 'sweetheart,' or 'darling,' just a casual affectionate term. Now I've picked it up. I like it.

She'd been in the office for forty-five minutes, and the time for daydreams was over. After calling Nan to arrange for a quick lunch, she went into the small conference room to find out what was going on.

"Hey, Angie, you look ready for anything!" Ken looked at her closely. Like many good lawyers, he was quick to notice moods and confidence.

"Thanks, so I've heard," she told him with a smile. "You all look concerned. Has anything happened to a client, or to one of the staff?"

Helen started, "Staff's fine. This is about a situation that affects the Filmore family. It could cause problems for us as well. Mrs. F. called yesterday, around noon, to tell us she was sending some paperwork by messenger from her lawyer's office. Said it would change what was in the file we have on power of attorney and health care proxy designations. Of course I gave it to Anne right away."

"They had their oldest daughter as primary for both, then Bill, the son, if she couldn't or didn't want to fulfill the responsibilities. Right?" Angie asked.

"Yes," Anne continued. "Well, Bill is off both documents as of now. They decided, because of his attitude, the younger daughter would be a better choice as alternate."

"OK. People have every right to adjust things. How is that bad for us?"

"Well, Angie, Mrs. F. called back around two." Ken took over the explanation. "His sister wanted to stick it to Bill, so she called and told him he no longer had authority to do anything for his parents. He went ballistic, went to her house and raised hell, shouting, even breaking a vase or two. She got scared, ran out and called 911. He tried to swat one of the cops who showed up, ended up cuffed in the back of the cruiser."

"What a jerk he is. The Filmores must be devastated," Angie commented.

"Oh yeah," Ken continued, "after some conversation, and finding out Bill had a clean record, the Desk Sergeant called the other daughter, who called the family lawyer. Everything got calmed down. Bill's probably pretty pissed though. Mrs. F. mentioned he said, quote, 'If Mom and Dad had gone into someplace like I wanted and not hired that bitch nurse, none of this would have happened.'"

"We got all that information late yesterday evening, but figured it could wait until you came in today. Bill was taken to the ER for chest pain after the episode. They kept him all night, so we decided you were safe," Anne told her boss.

"My god! I picked a bad time to desert you, didn't I?" She looked upset and guilty.

"Hey, Angie. You haven't taken time for yourself in god-knows-how-long. You deserve it. That's why we're here," Helen told her, adding, "I think he's just an obnoxious bully anyway."

"Maybe," Anne said, "He's vicious though. Wouldn't be surprised if he tried to sue us or something."

"And, that's why you all have me," said Ken. I know lawyers who deal with these matters all the time. I'm going to call the insurance company, just to give them a heads up."

Anne would call the Filmores to make sure they were OK and had everything they needed.

"Send out for lunch on me," Angie told them. "Call the Tavern for something really nice. You deserve it." The three thanked her as she went back to her office.

This isn't a good thing. Bill Filmore is a prominent business man around here. We don't need bad publicity. But then, he'll need to watch himself after being arrested. Too bad Charlie's away. I couldn't tell him the details because of confidentiality, but I could get a second opinion on possible legal implications.

She stopped herself mid-thought. Things might be different with Charlie now. *That's stupid. I've spent one weekend with Ben. Charlie's had other women the whole time I've known him. No reason we can't be friends now that I'm seeing someone.*

Helen knocked on the door. "Angie, phone call from Rita at the Council on Aging. She sounds excited about some new venture. Says you're going to love it."

"Sure. Put her through." Rita was a new director with progressive ideas about making life easier for the older population of Rock Harbor. "Hi, what's going on? Helen said you were enthusiastic about something."

"Am I ever! Have you heard about a program that creates kind of a condominium without walls for older people who want to stay in their homes instead of moving? It's up and running in Boston."

"Yes, I have, it's a great solution to find help taking care of everything that goes into managing a house. I think the company even arranges theater and concert trips. Do you think there's a chance for something like it to work here?"

"I've talked to Maureen, the Council director in Plover Cove. We're going to start a planning group to explore a joint venture. Will you join us?"

Angie thought for a minute. *Do I really want to take on another project? It won't be an easy task. Some people around here don't embrace new ideas. But, why not?*

"Sure, Rita. Helen has my schedule. Call her with some times that are good to meet, and she'll set it up. Thanks for including me."

I reentered work mode at full speed today. Haven't had a second to catch my breath. For the first time since she could remember, she would have liked another day to herself. She looked forward to lunch with Nan.

CHAPTER 35

NAN REACTS

N an waved from a small booth for two at Primo's, one of their favorite café-coffee shops. When Angie sat, there were already two large salads with cups of steaming soup on the table. "I took a chance and ordered what you usually have after a weekend of celebratory eating," Nan told her. "You did take time to eat, right? I want to hear it all, especially the steamy parts." She smiled lasciviously.

"Thanks for ordering. I'll tell you about the trip, but not everything. I don't kiss and tell." She gave Nan a snarky grin and took a spoonful of fragrant chicken soup. "Yes, smart-mouth, we did take time to eat."

"Angie, you're being a pain in the ass. You look refreshed and happy, though. Did you have a good time?"

"That's putting it mildly." She leaned closer to Nan across the table. "We like the same museums, he's a news junkie, and there was never a lull in conversation. We even had an argument because he's been stupid about an old girlfriend's motives. He was OK with me giving him hell."

Nan stopped eating. "Want to tell me about that?" her voice had an edge. "What kind of stupid?"

Angie gave her a thumbnail sketch about Ben's condo sitting arrangement, Ollie's scheme, and the aftermath. Skeptical as she was prepared to be, Nan reluctantly smiled at the whole thing. "Men can be so goddam stupid. Nobody could make that up. Even I believe him. So, I assume you two got to know each other again, in every way." It wasn't a question.

"Yes, we did." Angie smiled. "We were in a gorgeous suite at the Wellington. It had a separate bedroom for me. He made sure of that. "Then," she shrugged, "there's no other way to put it, I seduced him."

"Good for you, Angie!" Nan reached over and squeezed her arm.

"Nan, I'd forgotten how wonderful being loved like that could be. I felt sexy and cherished. Tried to keep reminding myself that we're different people from what we were years ago, but everything, not just the lovemaking, felt so right."

"You say lovemaking, not having sex."

"Yes," she sat back, looking thoughtful. "Because sex is fun, but making love is different. We took time to do all we could to please each other." Angie put her fork down and leaned toward her friend. "I'm scared, Nan. This started because I wanted closure. Now, it looks like I've opened a door instead of closing anything."

"You're wise to be scared. You loved him once. You probably have on some level for all the time he's been gone. Be careful, but don't let anything stop you from having a chance at what you really want." She looked directly into Angie's eyes. "Don't worry. I'll be keeping an eye on the

British Mr. Perfect. I plan to be brutally honest with you if I see any danger signals."

"You and Jake. We're having dinner with him and Eileen tonight. Ben met him that first night we went out and was thoroughly impressed."

"Good. Jake is a wise old fellow, and Eileen reads people well." She sat back and took the last forkful of her salad. "It must have been hard to come back to a daily routine after all of your adventures. Do you have a busy week?"

"Yeah, Nan. Maybe too busy. This morning was a bear. I'm thinking of taking myself off night and weekend call. It might be time to let Anne handle most of the day to day, too. She's had several well-qualified nurses submit resumes. Most want part time, which would work nicely. I'm busy with other aspects of the company. Of course, I'll stay involved on some level with the clinical side to be sure our clients continue to get the kind of service that's my brand."

Nan clapped her hands softly. "I do not believe I'm hearing this. Go for it, Angie. You're working sixty or more hours a week." *Even if it doesn't work out with Ben, Charlie'll be very happy to fill any extra free time you're willing to give. I think he really does care about you, and he'd probably make you happy. Much as I hate to say it, though, if Ben is the one, well, so be it.*

They hugged goodbye after their quick lunch. Angie headed back to the office to work on plans to cut her hours. Stopping into Anne's office, she asked, "Do you have a few minutes to have coffee and conversation with me around three?"

They finalized a new schedule. "OK, then. We have off hours covered, with backup in case of a sick call. This is a good move for you Angie. It's about time."

As usual, the rest of the day passed quickly. Suddenly, she realized it was only forty-five minutes before dinner at Jake and Eileen's.

Ben rang the bell fifteen minutes after Angie arrived home. He hugged her tightly, and his kiss was slow and thorough, but gentle. "You look as if you've had a busy day, my love."

After kissing him back, she said, "It was tough today, Ben. Do I look awful?"

He answered with another longer kiss. "That is impossible. Fix your lipstick and let's go before I do anything more to muss you up."

⚔┼┼⚔

Eileen greeted each of them with a hug. Ben had to bend almost double to return it. Jake was at her side seconds later, enveloping Angie in his big arms and firmly shaking hands with Ben.

"You've met Jake," Angie said. "This beautiful lady is Eileen Hughes, his wonderful partner."

"Lovely to meet you, Eileen. No doubt you know, I'm an old friend of Angela's." He handed her two bottles of wine, one red, the other white.

"Thank you so much, Ben. I hope you like a very traditional dinner. We're having roast beef."

"The aromas are wonderful. Sounds like the perfect meal for an autumn evening, Eileen. What can I do to help?"

Angie was happy that he offered.

"Well, maybe you and Jake can work on drinks. Everything else is pretty much ready. I want to show Angie a dress I bought. We'll be right there."

"Scotch for you ladies OK?" Jake asked.

"Perfect," the two women answered.

"Ben, I have some single malt choices here. I'd recommend Scapa."

Ben looked surprised and pleased. "Not a lot of people know that brand, Jake. You're a true Scotch drinker, I think"

Upstairs, Eileen took a white bag on a hanger from a closet. The long yellow silk dress shimmered. It was simple, proportioned to fit Eileen's petite frame perfectly.

"It's what I plan to wear for our Commitment Ceremony, Dear. I was thinking, don't you have a short forest green silk dress? It would look lovely when you stand with us as our witness."

Angie's eyes teared a bit with happiness. "It's one of my favorites. Of course that's what I'll wear."

"Ben is charming, Dear," Eileen said as she carefully hung the dress in the cedar closet, "Did you have a nice weekend?"

"Yes, Eileen. I followed your advice too. I didn't make him wait. Mostly because I didn't want to either. I'm afraid we might be getting too close too fast, though. It's been only a week since we've reconnected."

"You were physically separated, but was he ever totally out of your soul? For that matter, were you ever out of his?"

Angie had no words as they went to join the men.

Ben thoroughly enjoyed listening to Eileen and Jake tell him about Angela's work and how well regarded she was in the community. They congratulated him on his sons' venture and, without seeming to pry, found out a great deal about him and his businesses.

Eileen served Caesar salad for the first course, with anchovies on the side. Ben, Angie, and Eileen finished the plate. They laughed at Jake wrinkling his nose at the small fish. He did better eating a first and second helping of rare roast beef with twice-baked potatoes and asparagus. Ben poured the red wine he brought, along with another equally delicious one Eileen had on hand. The four decided to pause before dessert.

"Have you moved everything here now, Eileen, in preparation for renting your house?" Angie asked. "I've told Ben about your plans."

"Congratulations on the joyous celebration," Ben told them. His smile was warm and genuine.

They both thanked him. "You're welcome to join us if you have the time," Eileen said. "Angie is our witness. She can give you the details."

"It would be my honor."

"As for the move," Eileen continued, "we're working on it. If Liliana can rent the house furnished, there's not much to do. If not, I'll need to pack more and put things in storage. I don't want to trash kitchenware and good furniture. She's away this week on a vacation that was cancelled and then rescheduled at the very last minute."

"Yes," Angie responded, "She and Charlie are on a cruise. She told me all about it a while ago. Said she wouldn't need to pack much."

Eileen laughed. "I wasn't going to mention that little detail, but Lily does enjoy dropping small shockers. I assume she told you about the 'clothes optional' venues."

"Yes she did," Angie looked amused and just a bit annoyed at the same time.

Ben was all ears. "Was that the real estate woman at the club last Sunday when my friends and I crashed the party?" He asked.

"That's the one." Angie told him.

"She's on a cruise with your friend Charlie?"

"He has friends for different occasions. However, he's been saying it's time for him to settle down with a special friend," Eileen commented.

Jake laughed uproariously. "I wouldn't hold my breath for that to happen, Darlin'. He's a great guy though. Would give you the shirt off his back if he liked you."

"Hmmm." Angie responded.

Ben tried to keep a straight face.

He took a sip of wine and told Jake and Eileen, "I'm looking for at least a winter rental, or even longer, here or in Plover Cove. A furnished house would be perfect. It's just me, maybe my sons with a friend or two now and then, and perhaps another guest of whom I'm sure you'd approve. Could I put in a rental application?"

Eileen looked at Angie. "What do you think, Dear? Would Ben make a reliable tenant?"

After hesitating long enough to make Ben squirm a bit in his seat, she responded, "Yes, I'd trust him that way." He noticed she didn't elaborate on further areas of trustworthiness.

"Then, Ben," Eileen said, "take a look at the house. If you like it, the rent is twenty-five hundred a month for a year. We'd have to talk to Liliana about a shorter term, if that's what you want. I'd include snow removal and landscaping, of course. Utilities are separate, and will be the renter's responsibility. The location is good. You can see the harbor from the second floor."

"Sounds fine. I'll get in touch with Liliana when she returns. She gave me her card last week." He avoided looking directly at Angela, sensing her surprise that Liliana made a connection with him so quickly.

"No need to wait," Eileen said, "give me your number and I'll have someone from her office get in touch with you tomorrow."

After coffee and an apple tart, the four commented on how much they enjoyed the evening and said goodnight.

Watching the younger couple cross to Angie's house, Jake asked Eileen, "what do you think, Darlin'?"

"I can tell you like him, Jake, and so do I. It's obvious he makes Angie happy. I hope things work for them as well as they did for us."

He leaned down and kissed her. "I hope so too."

CHAPTER 36
MOVING ALONG

"Thanks for asking me along, tonight, Angela. They're a delightful couple. Hope I passed inspection. It was a bit terrifying, being vetted by two people who adore you."

"This wasn't an interview, Ben." She laughed at the idea. *You may not have thought so, my love, but it most certainly was.* "Well, it was encouraging when Eileen offered to rent her house to me, I guess."

"Ben, I'm absolutely exhausted," she told him when they got to her door. "Still, I don't want you to go."

"That's good to hear Angela, because I definitely want to stay with you. However, I'm dead tired too. It's been a long day, and I'm not a kid anymore." He put his arms around her loosely, "Would it be alright if we fell asleep just holding each other? Being together is all I really need. How about you?"

"Is that little overnight kit replenished with necessities?" she asked with a smile.

"Oh, yes. I'm an optimist." He got it from the trunk of his Land Rover.

Once in her living room, they shared a long hug and a quick kiss.

"Angela, please just put on whatever you usually wear to bed. Don't fuss on my account. I often sleep in my skivvies. Is that OK?"

"It's fine. Help me pull shades and lock up, and then we'll go upstairs. You can hang your things in the guest room. It has a bath attached. I'm going to grab a quick shower. Didn't have time before we went to dinner."

I'm taking him at his word about being comfy, although Nan would murder me for letting him see me in my huge and shapeless tee. At least this one is newish.

Ben thought she looked adorable in the oversized, yellow, crew neck tee shirt that came to her knees. He forgot how tired he was, but he had made a promise. They climbed into bed, and she nestled her head on his shoulder.

"Angela, it's ten-thirty. Would you keep an open mind about what we might do if we both wake up refreshed later? I promise, I wouldn't think of tempting you unless you wake up on your own with a similar thought."

She looked at him with a raised eyebrow. "Good night, Ben." She closed her eyes, then said softly, "That's not a bad idea though."

He fell asleep smiling.

For the first time in years, she didn't awaken for a solid seven hours. A full hour before the alarm, she slipped out of bed, used the bathroom, and took a finger full of toothpaste. Ben was coming back into the room when she returned.

"I slept like a log, Angela. Wonder if it was the mattress, or having you beside me? You smell like vanilla and spice."

"That's sweet. Cuddling with you definitely helped me to sleep, Ben. I'm usually up every couple of hours."

They came into bed again and spontaneously kissed each other gently. Then her hand lightly started to massage his tee shirt covered chest.

"Hmmm, that feels good." His eyes were closed and he sighed with content.

"Do you think we should sleep more?" she asked.

"Is that what you'd like to do?"

His hazel eyes were open now, and his hand moved over her back.

"Didn't we talk about other options if we woke up refreshed?" she teased.

When the alarm went off an hour later, sleep clothes were in a pile on the floor, and they dozed, happily entwined.

"Glad we kept an open mind, Ben." She stretched gracefully, covered only by the sheet.

He couldn't take his eyes off her body. "Would your open mind extend to a shower together, Angela?"

"Absolutely not! You have a bath in the guest room."

He chuckled. "Spoil sport. Take your time, my love. I smell the coffee. Do you want me to make you breakfast?"

"No, thanks. I don't eat until just before I leave, then it's just toast and peanut butter. Feel free to help yourself to anything you want. When I come down, I want to hear about the meeting with your sons and that company."

"Coffee's fine for me. I'll fill you in, and maybe we can discuss one or two other things too."

On the way to separate showers, they hugged tightly and shared a long kiss. She murmured, "Ben, you feel delicious and you're tempting me. But I really do need to be at work in two hours."

"Hmmm." He nuzzled her neck, restraining himself from letting his fingers wander. "OK. I get that. I'll behave. But only so you'll let me stay over on a work night again." He released her, reluctantly.

By seven, they were dressed and sitting in the kitchen. Over coffee, she heard the boys' deal with ICOS had made them multimillionaires, and it included the Cambridge house as part of a signing bonus.

"The meeting taught me some things about high tech business protocol. I knew not to wear a business suit," Ben told her, "but even wool trousers with a dress shirt and a sweater was too formal. Ryan and Pete introduced me as their 'senior consultant and backer.' Nellie was there too. At least she wore khakis, not jeans. I think Pete is head over heels in love. From the way she looks at him, it's mutual."

"You and the boys are good for each other, Ben. I'm so happy you approve of Nellie too."

"They're young adults, now, Angela. We respect each other's decisions on relationships and lifestyles."

She poured a second cup of coffee. "It's fun having you to talk to in the morning. You said you wanted to discuss something else."

"Yes. I promised I wouldn't try to monopolize your time. However, Ryan, Pete, Nellie, her dad, Mike, and his sister, Mae, are meeting me for brunch Sunday. Would you please come?"

"Ben, that sounds like a family thing. Is it fair to surprise them by including me? I'm not sure."

"Angela, I know it's been only about a week, eleven days to be exact, since we've reconnected. However, we're not young, and whatever happens, I want to make the most of the time we have with each other." He stood, took her hands and looked into her troubled eyes. "If that's too much too soon for you, well, I understand. I was the one who tore your heart apart. I'll deal with being just a new friend and an occasional lover for a while and hope you'll change your mind. I won't push you into anything." He moved back to his seat across the counter, then added, "You can be sure, however, I will not go away again unless we decide, together, it's the best thing for me to do."

Oh my god. All of this should be too much too soon, but I'm so happy. He's giving me time to trust him again. I might be a damn fool, but I'm not slowing things down anymore.

"Ben, you've changed my life in the last eleven days. So far anyway, it's been for the better. I don't feel that you're just a new friend, and I don't take occasional lovers. If you think meeting everybody on Sunday will be OK, then, I'll be happy to be there."

He saw a light mist of tears in her soft brown eyes. She stood, and they kissed sweetly and gently, the way they had in the parking lot at Vianni's.

"I'm going to be in Cambridge tonight, bunking in Ryan's guest room. Ollie took the few things I had at the condo, tossed them into a box, and sent it to the house. The boys and I are going for a three mile pre-dawn run and then to breakfast at some dive of their choosing. We've got several matters to talk about. I'm going to tell them a bit about us." He hugged her. "Can we see each other later in the week? Maybe you could help me organize some of my things at Eileen's house if it's ready."

"Sounds fine. I'll miss you."

"Me too, but more." He left with a wave.

Angie sat for a while over her toast and peanut butter. The house felt empty. *Nothing can stay this good. There are always hiccups. Ours are certain to come. Let's hope they won't be too bad.*

━═┽┾═━

Ben's phone rang just as he finished a run about eleven that morning.

"Good morning. It's Eileen. Jake and I enjoyed having you last night. Are you serious about considering my house to rent?"

"Last evening was my pleasure, Eileen. Thank you for letting me tag along. I definitely want to see your house, and as soon as possible. Angela must have told you I'm at the Washington Hotel in Salem temporarily."

He detected a smile in Eileen's voice. "Yes, she did mention that."

"Well, nice as it is, I'm sick of it."

"The realtor filling in for Liliana can show you the house at two this afternoon, if that works."

At two sharp, Ben was looking at a gray-shingled, two-story cape house on a small lot with a patch of well-tended autumn garden. Inside, he saw the rooms were smaller than Jake's, but not confining. The gray-blue color scheme reminded him of the ocean. Comfortable furniture sat on sparkling hardwood and slate floors. On the second floor, a window in the corner bedroom offered a harbor view. *This'll be a perfect office.* The larger of the other two rooms had a full bath just outside in the hall. A small but efficient looking kitchen was fully applianced, down to a coffee pot that made both a carafe and single serve. The three-quarter bath fitted into a custom extension off the first floor back hall. Small trees lined the sidewalks, and the area seemed quiet.

"I'll take it. If there are others who make an offer to pay more, I'll top it."

"Liliana was definite about requiring the first and last months' rent, as well as a security deposit."

"Not an issue." He told the nervous looking young man, "When can I sign the lease?"

"It will be ready by noon tomorrow, Mr. Whitcomb. You can move in on Saturday and Mrs. Hughes said there's no charge for these last two weeks in October." He'd feel better if he could run the two free weeks' thing by Liliana. *I hope it's OK, but Mrs. Hughes insisted. She seems to really like this guy. If there's a problem though, I'm the one who'll catch hell, as only Lily can dish it out.*

Around five, Ben got a text from Pete.

Dunk, I'm cookn. Can u do dinner here abt 7? Nellie asked if ud come.

He answered immediately.

Sure. Tx.

I'll pick up some champagne, just enough to do a little celebration of the deal, and for Nellie and Pete too. We won't drink much anyway, with the morning run coming up. The three of us haven't done one of those in months. Maybe I can slip something in about Angela and myself tonight so they'll have time to think about it before breakfast tomorrow.

CHAPTER 37
BEN'S SURPRISE

"Pete, I'm nervous." Nellie stood in the kitchen, with her deep blue eyes wide and her slender body tense.

"Nellie, Dunk thinks you're great. He's told us often how lucky we were to have you and your dad working on this house. Might have mentioned once or twice how pretty you are too, for a construction worker, that is." The young man brushed a strand of blond hair from her forehead, and hugged her. "Relax, Luv."

"Liking your designer is one thing, Pete, but finding out she's going to be living with your son is another. We should probably have told him a while ago we were dating. My Dad, too, for that matter." She rested her head on his shoulder.

"We fell in love pretty fast. Then it seemed daft for you not to be here, especially since you designed the perfect home for us. Damn good thing you and my brother like each other. Would've hated to have to buy him a place."

"You still use expressions from England, Pete. Nobody here says 'daft.' It's cute."

He was happy to see her smiling again.

She stayed in the circle of his arms and continued. "I feel like Ryan's my brother too. It'll be good to have him at dinner tonight. Your Dunk is a neat man. Dad doesn't make friends fast, but he and Ben really get along."

He rested his chin on the top of her head. "Sometimes I wonder what his life was like before he adopted us, Nellie. He never talked much about it except to say he had lived in Boston and liked it a lot. He and Julia, my step-mom, got along fine. They couldn't have been better parents, but Ryan and I weren't really blown away when they split. As we got older, we felt something was missing between them."

"You said they're still friends though."

"Oh yeah. Julia told us he made sure she'd never have to worry about money or a home as long as she lived. Not that there's any problem. She's very happy with her husband, and their little girl is a doll. We call her Sis."

She pulled away. "Pete, the Bourguignon smells delicious. I think it might be done."

"Just on time. I'll put the French bread in to warm. Your salad looks great, and the table's a masterpiece."

"Hey, you two ready for company?" Ryan called, knocking on the back hallway door. "Dunk's coming up the front stairs carrying flowers and something else."

When they opened the door, Ben handed Pete a white orchid plant and the champagne. He took Nellie in his arms for a hug and a warm kiss on the cheek. "He's a lucky fellow. I'm very happy for both of you."

Nellie returned his hug, and Pete could see her apprehension disappear. *Leave it to Dunk to make everything OK.*

The three men clapped each other on the back after Nellie took charge of Ben's gifts.

"Dunk, let me take your gear upstairs. You're dead set on this run tomorrow?"

"Sure am. You afraid I'll trounce you, Ryan?" he teased his son.

"Not so much. But don't worry, I'll set an easy pace."

"The flat looks beautiful, Nellie." He looked around approvingly. "I see your good taste and designer's eye everywhere. Dinner smells wonderful too."

"Pete gets credit for the main course, Ben. He lets me do salads and desserts. We buy fresh bread. Neither of us has the time or patience to make it."

"Don't overlook my contribution," Ryan broke in, "I'm very good at picking up wine and beer for when we eat together."

"When did you learn to cook more than the basic steak and lasagna, Pete?" Ben asked.

"Well, we mostly ate in the garage and lab while we worked on the Bots, and takeout got really old after a while. I remembered you used to make us tasty one-dish meals on top of the stove when Julia wasn't home and the housekeeper was off. Figured I might try them with a hotplate."

Ryan teased, "Yeah. Couldn't have been more surprised when nobody died from his cooking."

"You'd starve if we didn't feed you two or three times a week!" his brother shot back.

The four laughed over the easy banter between the young men. It was good to see Pete so self-confident and happy. Ben caught the discreet little touches his son and Nellie shared.

"Ben," she said, "I'm sorry Pete and I didn't tell you sooner that we were dating."

"Dating?" Ryan exclaimed. "He didn't look at another woman after the first coffee with you. First time in his life he made a decision on anything that fast. Damned if it wasn't the smartest one he's ever made too." He gave his brother a thumbs' up.

She blushed, reminding Ben of the way Angela reacted to compliments.

"No worries, Nellie. Sometimes things happen too fast for much advance notice. From where I sit, you two deserve a toast. Where's that champagne I brought?"

"Got it, Dunk." Ryan expertly uncorked the bottle and poured it into glasses.

"Speaking of Pete knowing right away that this lovely lady was for him," Ben remarked in a casual tone, "that might be a male trait in the Whitcomb line. Remember, you both have those genes on your mother's side."

"Really, Dunk?" Ryan asked. Both young men were suddenly attentive. "Do the men in the family have a history of falling in love quickly?"

Ben nodded, his smile mixing wistfulness with a touch of regret. "Yes, but some of us made a botched job of it, I'm afraid." He looked down for a second.

"I'd like to hear a bit more about that," Nellie said, not as reticent as his sons were to probe a little.

"Some got lucky. Even after behaving like complete clods, they got a second chance with the special lady."

Pete looked at his Dunk. "Did they do better the second time?"

Ben laughed, saying only, "One would hope so."

Ryan commented, "Well Dunk, it sounds as if there's some interesting family history we haven't heard yet. Will you tell us the stories?"

"It's kind of late for that tonight. But maybe soon."

The young people looked at him, all with a similar thought. *Something's going on, here.*

Nellie brought a special dessert of Bananas Foster to the table. "Since the three of you are running tomorrow, I thought it would be OK to have something really loaded with carbs tonight."

Ryan roared laughing. "So, this concoction of banana, ice cream, caramel, and nuts is really a health food?"

"For tonight, it certainly is," Ben told him.

The four spent several hours filled with wonderful food, laughter and good conversation. They drank little because of their morning plans. Although Nellie was invited to join them, she declined politely, saying, "The three of you will be competing and trying to annoy each other the whole time. I'll do Yoga instead."

At ten, Ben said goodnight. "Thank you for the great dinner, and the even better company." He kissed Nellie lightly on the top of her head. "See you guys on the porch at five-thirty." He headed upstairs to Ryan's guest room.

When they were cleaning up after dinner, Nellie asked the young men. "So, what was all that about the Whitcomb men falling in love fast?"

Both of them looked puzzled. "Don't know, Luv," Pete told her.

"Me neither," Ryan added. "That never came up before. He has me curious. Pete, do you remember last week, he mentioned meeting an old friend?"

"Yeah. When we asked him what was going on with Ollie. He very nicely told us to butt out."

"OK guys." Nellie said as she dried a pot. "I know men don't gossip about love lives and such, but he brought it up. Maybe he's ready to say more."

"You could be right, Luv. We'll sniff around a bit tomorrow."

As Nellie predicted, Ben and his sons alternated between a gentle pace, and sprints where they tried to outrun each other. The teasing was constant.

Ryan and Pete had planned a three-mile route up and down quiet streets, but made sure they were never more than a half-mile from the car. "Just in case one of us gets a cramp or something. It's a lot colder than running in Naples," they cautioned. Ben knew their strategy was for his benefit, and he was pleased at their concern. By the end of the run, he realized that keeping up with youngsters was challenging.

"Hungry, Dunk?" Pete asked.

"Yes. And ready to sit too."

Within minutes, they were at Mother's Diner ordering three egg omelets with double toast. A pot of coffee arrived on the table with a pitcher of water.

Ryan smiled up at the server, a pretty brunette with green eyes and a pleasant smile. "Thanks, Pam. We need this."

"You runners don't hydrate as much as you should. Drink that water before you chug the coffee."

"Sure thing, Ma'am," Ryan answered. His brother grinned.

"What, Pete? You look like an idiot with that smart-ass smile."

"Not a thing. Just haven't heard you so docile in a while."

They ate hungrily, with Pam replenishing their coffee and waters frequently.

"By the way," Ben told them, "I'm not homeless anymore. I've rented a place in Rock Harbor."

"Really? Isn't that where Ollie has her condo?" Ryan asked, finishing the last of his toast.

"Nope. It's the next town over. A pretty little spot, quiet in the winter. It'll be a good place to start the book. Close to the airport too. That'll be handy for Florida and London trips."

Pete commented, "Well, the North Shore is nice. We've sailed and surfed up there a couple of times. You can always crash in Cambridge if you need to be closer to Boston."

"I appreciate that, gents."

"Dunk," Ryan asked, "just curious. You and Ollie gotten together lately?"

"No. She wasn't very happy with me the last time we saw each other. She left without having dinner."

"When we were at the Fire Phoenix, you mentioned running into an old friend," Pete said. "That the reason Ollie's mad?"

Ben drank some coffee, then looked at both of them across the table. "OK, you two. I met my friend the first time twenty-five years ago, when I lived in Boston. Things didn't work out. My fault, not hers. Ran into her again fairly recently. We found out we still enjoy each other's company. Very much. Would you be comfortable if she comes to brunch Sunday? I'd like her to meet both of you, and Nellie too."

His sons weren't able to hide their surprise. They ignored the fresh coffee Pam just poured.

"Absolutely." Ryan responded.

"Of course," Pete told him.

"You think Nellie will mind?"

Pete chuckled. "Not a bit. She'll think it's great."

"Good. Angela was a little worried about joining a family celebration. I told her I thought you'd both be fine with meeting a very good friend of mine." His eyes twinkled when he said that.

Ryan asked casually, "She live on the North Shore?"

"Yes, she does," Ben answered, without elaborating.

They finished breakfast, and he picked up the check out of habit, over his sons' protests.

Back at the house, none of the men mentioned the surprise announcement until Ben went to shower. As soon as he was out of earshot, Ryan commented, "I think we know now why he told us that story about the Whitcomb men, Pete."

"Oh yeah." His brother answered. "Let's hope things work out this time."

CHAPTER 38

ANGIE'S PROBLEM

*B*en didn't make me feel uncomfortable for going to work instead of taking the morning off to spend with him. I don't know why that surprised me a little.

Angie was having trouble concentrating. She was trying to review material for a lunchtime presentation to a group of doctors about Concierge Nursing. Even though she'd been in the office for a couple of hours, it was hard to forget Ben's earlier feathery kisses and light nips. When she heard Helen on the phone, obviously concerned, she quickly snapped back to reality.

"Please, slow down a little. Oh, I am so sorry! She's right here. Let me get her for you immediately." Helen hurried into the office and said, handing her the phone, "A big Filmore crisis."

"Oh Angie, I never thought it would come to this," Mrs. Filmore said tearfully. "Our son came over this morning, originally to make peace. Well, next thing I know, Gus lost his temper about something, Bill started yelling, then Gus called 911 saying he was being threatened. Because it was the second report on Bill, our attorney couldn't smooth things over. The police are holding him. Angie. He's apparently been yelling that none of this would have happened if we hadn't met with you. Please be careful."

"I will, but are you both OK?"

"Yes. Our girls are here. They thought I should let you know what's going on."

"Thank you. Please don't worry about me. Take care of yourselves." Angie frowned as she hung up and buzzed her office manager.

"Helen, will you call Ken for me? We may have a legal problem after all. It's probably a good idea to keep the front door locked for a few days, and warn the staff that we have a family member who's furious with us."

"That's happened before, Angie."

"Yes, but this might be worse than usual. Without violating any rules of confidentiality, I can let Captain Scott at police headquarters know we'd appreciate some extra vigilance for the building."

The police captain took her call immediately. "Angie, this guy is pissed. He's been telling everyone that you put ideas into his father's head about something or other."

"Tim, that's not accurate. You know I can't say too much because of confidentiality."

"We don't need to know details, but there's nothing confidential about what he's thinking," Captain Scott told her. "His lawyer's pushing us to let him go again without charges. Not happening this time. He might impress a judge with apologies later, but he'll be in a cell for at least four more hours."

"Thanks, Tim. Let's hope that will make him rethink his temper tantrums."

"He'll probably be let go on personal recognizance with a stern warning. He's a business man in town and this'll be the second time he makes the paper. It might straighten him out. Still, watch yourself Angie."

"I will." When Angie hung up it was time to leave for the presentation. She was no longer distracted, but very focused on work.

By five-thirty, after a successful lunch seminar with several follow-up appointments scheduled, and bringing Ken and Anne up to date, she was tense and weary. *I think what I need to do is hit the gym tonight for an hour. It's been nearly a week and I haven't been careful with eating.* Nan was busy, so there'd be no temptation for wine afterward.

Angie was exhausted by ten. Ben had texted earlier. She missed the sound of his voice. *Get over it. He's not going to be with me every night. He lives in Florida part-time. There'll be weeks we probably won't see each other. This might not even work out, for godssake. But I feel more and more confident that we're meant to be.* She took a shower and was asleep in minutes.

⋘✠⋙

Ben texted her at eleven the next day.

Miss U. evrthng all good. Back aftn. Call me when u can. B.

She called him immediately. "Hi. How was dinner? Did the run go well?"

"Good morning, my love. Dinner was extraordinary. Pete loves to cook and he's excellent. He and Nellie are a team. They both enjoy Ryan, so the living arrangement is working. As for the run, well, the boys took good care of me. Made sure we were never far from the car and set a pace I could keep, even with the sprints."

"Great. How did it feel?"

"They're in their twenties. I'm just now recovering. By the way, I told the boys I wanted them and Nellie to meet you. They were excited you're coming to Sunday brunch."

"What did you tell them about me?"

"I described you as an old and very special friend. They may have drawn certain conclusions. Now, can we get together for dinner tonight?"

"Oh, Ben, I have a meeting with the Rock Harbor Women's Business Owners group."

"OK." He sounded disappointed. "Too bad, but those meetings are important."

She was pleasantly surprised at his reaction again, and almost told him to come by for a drink later, but stopped herself. *He seems to accept that he's not the only thing in my life. That's good.*

"I'm signing the lease for Eileen's today. She said I could move in Saturday. Any chance you'd like to help?"

"Of course I will. Nan and Jim asked if we wanted to meet them for dinner tomorrow night as well. Are you available?"

"Indeed I am," he said. "May I call you later tonight for details?"

"Please do. I should be home by ten. It'll be good to hear the sound of your voice before I sleep."

"Ten's not all that late," he said hopefully.

"Tomorrow's not that far away, either. Maybe you could get a second little bag and leave it in the guest room."

"Gladly, my love. Why don't you pack one for Eileen's? Only in case of something unforeseen that would keep you overnight of course."

"Ben, we're hanging up now, before this conversation goes any further." There was a smile in her voice.

"Oh, all right."

Just before the end of her day, Angie got a call from Captain Scott. "Filmore was released, but under court order to stay away from his father unless invited. One of his sisters or a lawyer needs to be there too. He has to attend an anger management program as well."

"That might work, Tim," she said.

"The judge gave him holy hell in open court, and local newspaper reporters were there. He looked scared out of his mind. If he screws up again, he'll get much more severe punishment. The judge made that clear."

"Thanks, Tim. Hope that's the last we hear of him."

Angie looked forward to her evening. She always enjoyed the women in the business group. This meeting would be less colorful than usual because of Liliana's absence.

"Anyone know where she went?" One of other women asked.

"No. But it's either a man or a deal." Someone answered.

"Maybe both if Lil's really on her game," the woman who owned a jewelry store commented. "I give her credit."

Angie couldn't help smiling.

Ben called just after she got home. "How was the meeting?"

"Good, as usual. Maybe not as much fun as being with you."

"Glad to hear that, Angela. You know I'm only minutes away if you want company."

"That's a tempting offer, but I'm already half-asleep. Tomorrow'll have to do."

"Hmmm. I don't have a choice. However, I do have something for you to consider. I need to attend a party in

Naples next weekend. Planning to leave on Friday and return Monday. I know this is last minute, but is there any possibility you could come with me?"

"Well, Ben, I might not be able to leave until late Friday, but I do like Naples, and I'd love to go."

He sounded delighted. "The weekend will be much more enjoyable with you there. What time should I pick you up tomorrow?"

"About seven. It feels like a while since we've seen each other. That's a silly thing to say, isn't it?"

"I'm so glad you noticed, Angela. It'll be two and a half days. Goodnight, my love."

CHAPTER 39
OLLIE'S ALERT

Angie was glad the last day of her workweek was progressing without more than the usual pre-weekend controlled chaos.

When she told Anne she was taking some time to visit Florida, it was fine. "Go, Boss. Have a great time. If you come back looking as good as you did from that Berkshire weekend, you should start your own blog on vacations that rejuvenate." She pretended not to notice Angie's light blush.

"Thanks. Since everything is well under control for a Friday, I'm going to leave a little early today as well."

On the way home, she stopped to pick up a bottle of Mumm's champagne for the following evening to celebrate Ben's move. *He'll most likely arrive early tonight as usual, but I still have time to shower and change.* Spritzed in Chanel and wearing soft lacy underwear, she put on dark brown straight leg velveteen pants. A soft copper-color pullover sweater with little hints of sparkly threads in the weave was perfect for the cool weather. Her diamond studs were a nice finishing touch to the glamorously casual outfit.

My life has changed so much in just two weeks. I've gone from a careful, grounded widow to having a sizzling romance with an old love. It might be the most idiotic thing ever, but he feels like a love I've always had.

She had just hung a nearly backless, slinky black satin nightgown on the bathroom hook when the bell rang. *No tee shirt tonight.*

When he was barely inside the door, Ben took her in his arms and held on as if he hadn't seen her in months. She clung to him the same way. They kissed each other lightly first, smiled and kissed again. This time, the longing they had built up over the few days apart exploded. Ben caught Angie when she moaned and he felt her knees buckle.

He whispered, "Well, my love. We could ring Nan and tell her something came up."

Angie went from weak at the knees to bubbling with laughter. "Ben, we can't cancel at the last minute. And we couldn't tell her what it was that came up, now could we?"

"You are a wicked woman, Angela, commenting on that." His eyes sparkled with suppressed laughter. "I, after all, did not remark on your inability to stay upright."

She hugged him once more, quickly, saying, "I'll make amends later."

"I shall look forward to that," he told her in a husky voice.

They arrived at the Plover Cove Tavern, laughing and holding hands.

Watching from their table, Nan smiled. "Jim, I remember them together, looking at each other that way nearly twenty-five years ago. Do you think this is an echo that will fade?"

She trusted her husband's ability to read people. He just pretended Ben got him drunk at the club a couple of weeks ago, she was sure. He did it to avoid discussing whatever they talked about.

"Hon, how would I know anything more than you?"

"Because, after seeing you and Ben at the Club, I've a feeling it wasn't the first time you talked since he left." Nan turned to face him, and squeezed his wrist, hard. "Don't tell me for sure, because I'd have to kill you if I thought you held out on anything about their break-up."

"Ouch! I'll have bruise marks." He smiled mysteriously at his wife while he pried her fingers away. "I think he realizes that Angie is the woman he's always loved. He'll do all he can to get a second chance. If she feels the same way, things should work out."

"So, Jim, you really think this time it could be forever?"

"I do, Hon." He kissed his wife lightly on the lips.

"Oh my goodness!" Angie greeted their friends, "It's nice to see an old married couple making out in public."

"Mouthy, isn't she?" Jim said as he hugged Angie and clapped Ben on the shoulder.

The two women gave each other a quick hug. Angie whispered to Nan, "Be nice."

"Humph. If he deserves it," Nan whispered back. She gave Ben a pleasant smile, but made no move toward a hug or a kiss on the cheek.

He followed her lead and smiled back. *She really would have no compunctions about doing me in if she thought my intentions about Angela were questionable. Not that I blame her.*

After the server took drink orders, Nan asked Ben, "How do you like being in this area?"

"I've enjoyed my short stay enough to have rented a little house in Rock Harbor for a while."

Jim caught his wife's look of surprise. He guessed she and Angie hadn't talked about that yet. Nan was out of town for most of the week at an art course. He didn't let her comment, saying "The off-season is nice here, Ben, especially if you escape the snow and ice with some time down south."

From just behind the server as he brought drinks, the foursome heard a vibrant female voice. "Well, how nice to see you Ben. Looks like you made some friends while you lived in my condo."

The other three caught a slight grimace, quickly replaced by a smile, as Ben stood. He tactfully avoided a full hug by taking the striking woman's elbows before she could wrap her arms around him.

Ollie wore a black scoop-necked cashmere sweater over well-tailored olive wool slacks. The loose pile of darkest brown curls and tan leather boots finished her casually elegant look. As usual, she kept jewelry at a minimum, wearing only massive gold earrings. Her dazzling smile enveloped the whole table.

Nan and Angie had the same reaction. *No wonder he ran away at one in the morning when she showed up. This lady gets what she wants.*

Jim sat, fascinated at the tableau. *Wow! He certainly has some interesting folks in his life.*

Nobody noticed the tall, dark-haired young man who came to stand beside Ollie, until he said, "Hi, Ben."

Nan gave them an admiring once-over. *They're both over six feet. She's heavy, but still gorgeous. They look like a photo shoot advertising the perfect couple.*

"Franco! This is a pleasant surprise." Ben sounded relieved.

"Franco? Not Gino's son Franco?" Angie stood to face him with a warm smile.

"Yes, I am." He studied her face. "Angela? Uncle Ben's beautiful friend? Oh my god, it's been a very long time!"

He turned to Ollie. "I was ten years old and I had a huge crush on this gorgeous lady. She always treated me like the most special kid in the world when they came to the restaurant."

Taking Angie in his powerful arms for an affectionate hug, he missed the shock of realization on Ollie's face.

She tugged at his elbow saying, "Our table is probably ready. Nice to meet everyone." She looked straight at Ben, adding, "I understand things now."

Franco stopped her. "Ollie, I think you might want to mention something to Ben before we sit."

"Oh yes." She looked down and then faced him. "Remember at the Four Seasons a couple of weeks ago? When I pushed you into being my date for the pre-game party?"

"Yes, I remember it vividly." He smiled. "I met Angela that afternoon for the first time in years."

"Well, a photographer took our picture together. It'll be in the Boston paper's Society Section on Sunday. The editor called me for more information about us. I had a bruised ego, so I may have exaggerated some things just to annoy you a little."

She looked at Angie who was sitting with a pleasant, but unsmiling face. "It was a stupid thing to do. I explained everything to Franco a few days ago. He told me I needed to tell you too. Unfortunately, I couldn't, because you never answered my texts and I knew you wouldn't want me relaying anything through Ryan or Pete."

"OK, then," Franco interjected. "We didn't want you to be surprised, Ben. Dad and I would love to have all of you as our guests for dinner any time," He wrapped a protective arm around Ollie and kissed her cheek as they went to their table.

"Well, there's a little drama to start the evening. She's got that kid wrapped around her finger. Good luck to him," Nan remarked with a touch of acid in her voice.

Just then, the server reappeared with another round of drinks. "From the couple who stopped by your table. The gentleman said to bring these right away."

Jim raised his glass. "To Ben, the toast of society. Can't wait to see the picture!"

Ben noticed Angela was smiling, but not saying anything. *It would be awful if she had seen that damn photo without warning. Ollie didn't say why she had a bruised ego. That woman can cause trouble even when she doesn't intend to.*

"Ben. You're a million miles away." It was Angela, pulling him back into the conversation.

He took her hand under the table. "No, I'm not," he said very softly. "I'm here with you, exactly where I want to be."

"Hey, I'm starved. Can we eat, please?" Nan's comment lightened the mood.

The evening went by quickly, with lively conversation. Nan's attitude toward Ben thawed, especially when she heard he had invited Angie to Florida for the weekend.

"So, are you going Angie?" she asked.

"Well, he's promised me a party. How could I refuse?"

He laughed. "It's an obligation, really. I'm on the Symphony board, and we do a black-tie thing before the holidays. Thought Angela might like to meet some nice people and get a little sun."

"Black-tie, Ben?" She turned toward him, frowning thoughtfully. "You didn't mention that. I'll need to give some thought to a dress."

Nan made a mental note to make a few phone calls to her artist friends in Naples about this party. *I can help with the dress when I know more.*

"Would you like to come to the house for an after dinner Irish Coffee?" Angie asked their friends.

"We'll take a raincheck, Angie. I was doing sixteen-hour days at the Art Institute this week. Still trying to recover. OK with you, Jim?"

"Sure, Hon. Thanks for asking though, Angie."

The women hugged and Nan whispered, "Make him do penance for that picture."

"Interesting idea," she whispered back.

CHAPTER 40

ANGIE GETS EVEN

B en kissed Angie when he helped her into the Land
Rover. He thought she returned it, but with puckered
lips. *We are in a public parking lot, I guess. I'd have liked a more
enthusiastic response.* He turned on a soft-rock tape, and the
ten-minute ride home was more silent than usual. She did
reach for his hand. *That's a good sign.*

In her driveway, he turned toward her. "Angela, I am
sorry Ollie surprised us with that announcement tonight.
She can be a drama queen. I told you that before."

"Yes, and you didn't exaggerate. I just never pictured
her as such a gorgeous woman. She's quite young too."

"She's in her forties."

"Well, you should definitely be flattered that her ego
was bruised because of something or other you did or didn't
do." She didn't smile and wouldn't meet his eyes.

"Angela, I realize you might be a bit unsettled. But please
don't send me away tonight. I'll stay out of your way if you
like, you won't even know I'm here. If you just want to think
about all this, let me bring you hot chocolate and tuck you

in. Ask whatever you like, and I'll answer. But don't shut me out." He squeezed her cold fingers.

She looked at him. "Did you bring a bag to leave in the guest room?"

"Yes. I dropped it inside the front door. You didn't notice, I guess."

"No, I was a bit distracted. Let's go in. First, please put your car in the garage."

"Sure. You haven't asked me to do that before. I'm curious why."

"No need to advertise when I have a guest, Ben." *No need to tell you someone might be out to damage anything around me, either.*

She got out of the car and used a key to open the garage door, closing it after he parked.

In the front hall, she didn't hug him, saying, "Hot chocolate sounds good. Can you whip cream too? Do I need to show you where everything is?"

"I'll find what I need. May I bring a cup to drink with you?"

"I guess." She looked away. "You're being very thoughtful. You've done nothing wrong you know. I was just taken aback by seeing Ollie for real."

Hope he's OK when he finds out I'm setting him up. Serves him right for not telling me about the photo.

Twenty minutes later, he was in his shirtsleeves, tapping lightly on her half-closed door with a tray in his hands.

"Come in." Her voice was throaty. She was sitting on the bed, facing away from him. He could see her back, naked to the waist, in a black gown that clung like a second skin. Her vanilla and spice fragrance perfumed the air.

"Angela?"

"Do you have the chocolate, Ben?"

"I do."

"Is there lots of cream?"

"There is." His voice was hoarse.

"Good." She stood and walked toward him. He saw two wide strips of satin for the front of her gown, held loosely by thin straps. It slipped a bit, exposing the sides of her breasts when she reached for a cup.

"Angela! What the hell are you trying to do to me?" He could barely speak. "I'm going to drop the tray."

Sipping some chocolate, and then licking her lips, she said. "Put it on the dresser."

He did as he was told, with shaky hands.

"You were the one who wanted to have a cup with me while I thought about things."

She had a little whipped cream mustache. He took her cup, put it on the tray, and licked the top of her lip.

She grasped his hands, staring into his eyes. "Ben, please don't bruise my ego like you did to Ollie. Stay here."

The buttons of his shirt opened easily under her hands. Kissing her, he ran his fingers the length of her back and slipped his thumbs under the sides of the gown to caress her breasts.

She cried out in delight and unbuckled his belt, brushing him lightly. He gasped, pulled off his trousers, and kissed her again, deeply this time, their tongues dancing. He turned her away from him feather-kissing her from neck to ankles as he gently pulled the silky sheath to her feet. While he tugged at the rest of his clothes, she turned and flicked her tongue over his body. His knees almost buckled.

In bed, they teased, and touched and kissed, prolonging the sensual ache of wanting each other.

When Ben's eyes were hazel pools of fire, she whispered, "Please, my darling, love me. I want you so much."

This time, their passion had the power of waves crashing at high tide. Light scratches from her nails excited him. His mouth and tongue set her on fire. He didn't hold back, and she pushed him further with her shudders and screams of delight.

Neither of them knew how long they made love, but when it was over, they were lying, skin to skin, too exhausted to move.

"Angela, you are an exquisite lover. Did I hurt you? I'm afraid I lost control for a minute or two. Are you all right?"

"You are more than exquisite. I'm glad you lost control. It's never been like that for me. I'm a little embarrassed about screaming." She buried her face in his neck.

He rubbed her back. "Don't ever worry about what you do with me, my love. As long as it gives you pleasure, it's all beautiful and right."

They kissed, softly this time, then slept, wrapped around each other.

Ben awakened to coffee smells, and the aroma of something baking. He was a bit stiff and areas of his back smarted a little. *Ahhh, yes. She made me nearly mad with wanting her. And she planned it. I'll bet it was her revenge for that photo. She's full of exciting surprises.*

A damp towel and the light smell of lavender told him she had showered. He used the guest room to do the same. Dressed, he found Angela, without makeup; in a loose shirt and flannel pants. She was at the stove, cooking what seemed to be quiches.

"Good morning." Her face glowed as she greeted him. "Thought I'd have to go up and drag you out of bed."

"Good morning, what?" He asked her, standing in the kitchen doorway, smiling.

CHAPTER 41

THE DECISION

"Sorry? What do you mean, good morning, what?"

"Last night you called me darling, Angela. That's what you called me when you finally decided we were in love a quarter of a century ago."

She looked at him, startled, and was quiet for a minute. He didn't move.

"Ben, please don't start trouble." She concentrated on fiddling with the oven controls. "It's two weeks to the day since we met. Originally, I thought we might get to a quick good night kiss if anything at all by now."

"Ahh, but we haven't got a lifetime anymore, my love." He walked over and put his arms around her. Her lips looked a tiny bit bruised.

"Oh my god. Your lips. I did hurt you last night, didn't I? Are they terribly sore? I am so sorry, Angela." He held her gently and kissed her forehead.

"Ben. I've been eating some blueberries. I'm fine."

"Oh thank heaven! Then I can kiss you."

"Wait. Only If you tell me something first." She put her hand on his chest.

"Yes?"

"You've always called me 'my love.' Is that a cute British equivalent of 'sweetheart', or 'honey'?

"No, Angela. It means I think of you as my love. I've never used it with anyone else."

Her mouth opened to comment, but she was at a loss for words.

"Now, may I kiss you?"

"Please do... Darling."

"Angela..."

"Don't ask questions, Ben."

Sirens, becoming louder, interrupted their embrace. The phone started to ring at the same time.

There was a commotion in Angie's driveway and someone pounded on her front door.

They both rushed to open it. A Rock Harbor police sergeant greeted her.

"Ms. Martin-Wilson, a neighbor spotted this guy skulking around your car. Called us, then took matters into his own hands. Something we discourage, even if he handled it OK."

Jake was standing in the driveway with a small gun in his hand. He frowned at a terrified looking and handcuffed young man sitting on the ground.

Another cruiser arrived. Captain Scott got out, shouting. "Jake, what the hell did you think you were doing, flashing that gun?"

"Timmy, for chrissake, I have the permit for it. You know that."

"Yeah, and we should've pulled it a long time ago, you old coot."

"Well, this clown seemed to respect what it could do. He behaved very nicely when I told him not to touch the tires with that pick, or he'd be missing something important."

"Put the damn thing away, Jake, OK?" Captain Scott was annoyed.

"You know this guy, Angie?" He asked.

She shook her head no, but looked frightened. Ben could feel her tremble when he put his arm around her shoulders.

Eileen had come out, as well as a few neighbors. Someone said that a couple of other cars had been vandalized over the last few days.

"Don't worry," the Captain said to Angie, "I doubt it has anything to do with Filmore. He went into alcohol rehab right after court the other day. Guess he had a problem. I'm pretty sure he's getting straightened out."

Ben said nothing, but knew he'd ask about this Filmore, whoever he might be.

Within minutes, Jake, Eileen, Ben and Angie were sharing coffee and flavorful quiches around her table.

"Jake, you promised me you'd never use that damn gun." Eileen's voice was sharp.

"And I didn't, Love. Just showed it to the little twit."

The two women just looked at him, stunned at the old man's audacity. Ben hid a smile.

"It's sometimes handy to have one around, Jake. How often do you practice?"

"At least once a month, Ben. You're welcome to come along whenever you want."

"Thanks. I have a permit to carry in Florida, but not here. Would they let me borrow a pistol at the range?"

"No, but as my guest, there'd be no problem with you shooting mine."

"If I didn't love you so much, Jake, I'd smack you, trying to involve Ben in your shenanigans," the pretty little woman told him.

"Understandable," Angie murmured. *He never mentioned owning a gun. Wonder why he thinks he needs it?* She changed the subject. "How are plans for the ceremony, you two?"

"Everything's in place for November first," Eileen told her. "That's in two weeks. Ben, are you moving in today?"

"Yes, and Angela's going to help. There's not a lot to do, Eileen, because you've left the place pristine and very well furnished."

"We'll, we'd better let you get to it," Jake started to stand, but Ben stopped him.

"Wait a sec, I need to give you a heads up about something you might see in Sunday's paper."

Angie was surprised, and very pleased that he was going to explain about the picture.

"Afraid I got myself in a bit of a spot," he told the couple. By the end of the story, they were both having trouble keeping a straight face.

"Ben," Jake said as he got up, "I'm really glad you let us know. If you didn't, I might have taken this gun out for the third time in twenty years. The story will be around town in minutes after the paper comes out, I'm sure. Might want to tell Charlie when he gets back, Angie, before he tries to punish someone he thinks might have deceived you."

After they left, Ben turned to her and asked, "Want to tell me about Filmore?"

She burst into tears, showing the results of the morning's fear and stress. He held her against his chest. Finally, she gave Ben the gist of the matter, adding that she couldn't tell some details because of confidentiality.

He had his arm around her as they sat on the couch. "Is that the reason you wanted my car out of harm's way, Angela?" His voice was terse and low.

"Yes, Ben."

He moved away from her. "I am angry with you for not telling me you could be in danger. I am quite angry, actually. Did you tell Jake, or Nan, or Charlie, or anyone else?"

"Oh, Ben. I didn't want to involve people in my work troubles."

He stood with his back toward her, and his face was stern when he finally turned.

"It was selfish and cruel to keep something like that from people who care about you. Nobody would have known to keep an eye out for anything unusual going on around the property or even thinking about making sure you were safe working late."

"Ben, I did involve the police. I'm not a complete idiot."

His face looked haggard. "I would make it my mission in life to do great harm to anybody who hurt you Angela. I'm leaving now to cool down for a bit."

She responded with a tight voice. "Fine. Good thing you didn't have that gun you never told me about with you. You may have shot that kid even though Jake had the good sense not to. I assume you won't need my help this afternoon."

He heard her voice crack and stopped at the door. "Angela. You scared me by putting yourself in danger. I reacted. It's a disagreement, not the end of us. Of course I want your help moving in this afternoon."

She couldn't hold back tears. He went to her and sighed. "You still can't believe I'm in for the long haul, can you? Well, listen. I've never stopped loving you, and I realized it the second I heard your voice that morning two weeks ago. I'll never try to run your life, but I do hope you'll let me be a part of it." He sat on the couch, putting his arm around her shoulder again.

"I know it will take some time for you to trust me completely, considering how I botched things before. However, if you know for certain you can never give us another chance, please tell me and send me away. Otherwise, I'm staying, as maddening as you can be."

She got up and stood looking at him. "I've already made a decision about what I want to do about us, Ben."

He appeared calm, hiding a heart that pounded and a wrenching gut.

"Are you sure you've given yourself enough time, Angela?"

She reached down, taking both his hands in hers, and looked straight into his eyes as he stood.

"How much time for a decision like this is enough? Are there ever guarantees? All I know is that I love you too. Probably always have as well, because this doesn't feel new. I have no doubt that you're the one I want to be with for as long as I live. You're right, Ben. We shouldn't waste any more time."

"I feel exactly the same way, but are you positive my love?" he asked, studying her face.

"I am, Darling. We'll just enjoy what we have, and figure things out as we go along. We've both had a lot of experience doing that."

"A perfect plan," Ben agreed.

They held each other closely and kissed for a long time, both looking forward to their future.

Thank you for reading *This Time Forever.* I hope you enjoyed the story.

If you would take the time to leave a review on Amazon, it will be much appreciated. Writing just a short sentence, or even a few words is fine.
Web site is: www.amazon.com

Thanks again,
Mary

ABOUT THE AUTHOR

Mary Cooney-Glazer found a second career writing fiction. She is a firm believer that over forty does not mean immune to romance, and enjoys telling stories about adults with life experience who discover new love. Her special niche is writing light, warm, and optimistic reads. Of course, there is always a dash of something difficult in the plot to keep things interesting.

She often incorporates her background as a Registered Nurse into her stories. She has published short works on line, and is a member of Romance Writers of America and North Shore Scribes.

Mary lives north of Boston with her patient husband, an always-brewing pot of coffee, and an old, spoiled-rotten, noisy cat. Currently, there's another book in the works about some people who know Ben and Angie.

She welcomes hearing from readers and other writers alike.

Contact Mary Cooney-Glazer

Email: mcgbooks@aol.com

Made in the USA
Columbia, SC
26 May 2018